mission impossible . . .

"Whiskey, did you happen to see who the captain of the Secret Police ship was?"

"They called him Webern."

"Captain Webern? How nice. He's an old friend from my training days. The benefit of fighting against old friends is that you know all their weaknesses. I think that's going to come in handy now. I'm sure they're going to be curious about the information at this stage. Even if they didn't manage to get its importance from Dr. Pablo, our involvement in the affair will unfortunately spark the chief's interest. But what if they follow the doctor's instructions, thinking that they are going to have what the old man keeps calling the most devastating weapon ever created . . . what if they excitedly do all this and the experiment fails? What would they think then?"

"They'd think the old man was off his rocker," Whiskey mused, following Deadalus's reasoning.

"Exactly. If they carefully follow Pablo's instructions and come up with nothing, they'll think that the good doctor must have been having an old man's fantasies of Armageddon. They'd shelve the whole thing and never think of trying to recreate the experiment from scratch."

"What you're saying is that we should somehow replace the doctor's information with fabricated figures."

"Right. Or, if possible, just alter some of the key figures so that everything still looks the same but that the results flop."

"Wonderful idea, Captain, only it seems nigh impossible."

"Of course," Deadalus grinned at Whiskey's skepticism. "Everything we've done so far has been . . ."

Also by Symon Jade:

STARSHIP ORPHEUS #1: RETURN FROM THE DEAD

SYMON JADE

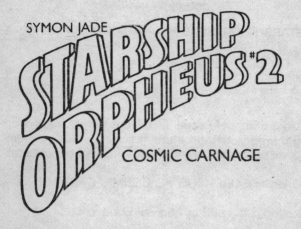

STARSHIP ORPHEUS #2

COSMIC CARNAGE

PINNACLE BOOKS   ℗   **NEW YORK**

STARSHIP ORPHEUS #2: COSMIC CARNAGE

Copyright © 1982 by Michael Eckstrom

An original Pinnacle Books edition, published for the first time anywhere.

First printing, April 1983

ISBN: 0-523-41647-4

Cover illustration by Earl Norem

Printed in the United States of America

PINNACLE BOOKS, INC.
1430 Broadway
New York, New York 10018

COSMIC
CARNAGE

chapter one

Deadalus yanked and the small compartment slid belligerently open. He took out a liter-sized plastic containter that seven months earlier had been full with dark rum. He held it up to the ceiling light and shook it, squinting. There were five or six ounces left.

Captain Deadalus hesitated. When the rum was gone he'd have to resign himself to the artificial powdered beer.

Sighing, he put the rum away and sat back down in front of the display terminal. He reread the message.

Alter course to Meer. Pick up Dr. Pablo from local police. Take all steps necessary to obtain information.

—Hissler.

The chief of the Empirical Secret Police had not meant the message for Deadalus, of course. The instructions had been sent in code from the home office on Earth to a starship in a nearby sector.

Deadalus had no trouble breaking the code. No more than he had with any of the codes they'd developed since he had *retired* from the service.

The message interested Deadalus. Dr. Pablo was an old friend. One of the most respected microbiological engineers, Pablo worked extensively for the Secret Police. That was where Deadalus had met him. How had he so quickly fallen on the bad side of the powerful agency? The doctor had always been an intelligent and honorable person. Which is probably why he had run afoul of the police force. Anyone with honor did, sooner or later.

Deadalus's curiosity was piqued. The *Orpheus* was close to Meer and he wanted to go down and check out the situation. Maybe lend a hand to an old friend.

There were some problems with this, however. Though Deadalus had the advantage of using the equipment on the starship *Orpheus* to listen in on all the Secret Police's communications, this advantage was neutralized by the fact that they knew he could. The message could be false. It could be a trap. It didn't seem all that likely. But Deadalus knew firsthand that the SP specialized in unlikely methods.

Grimacing, Deadalus gave in and got the

rum back out, pouring half of what remained into a small plastic glass.

He was going to have to chance it, if for no other reason than to find out if it was in fact a trap. If the SP was feeding him false information, the sooner he found out the better.

Besides, Meer produced the best fruit brandies in the entire galaxy.

"Laser generator?"

"Full."

"Rockets?"

"Five primed. Three in waiting."

"Alright, Whiskey, looks like we're ready to go."

Whiskey nodded and called the bridge on the landing craft's radio.

"Ready for separation, Jay."

"Rightio. One-three-three degrees declension. And off you go."

There was a sudden jerk as the landing craft separated from the mother ship.

"Landing craft *Ezra*, separation completed. You're on your own."

"Thanks, *Orpheus*. See you later."

"Call when you need us."

Deadalus couldn't suppress his grin. Jay and Whiskey sounded like they were exchanging greetings on a street corner. It was a far cry from the rigid and specialized language they used on the police force. But, he noted with pride, the separation maneuver had gone as perfect and graceful as a ballet step.

Seven months ago the crew of the *Orpheus*

had been nothing more than a half-starved group of criminals and political misfits. That was when Chief Hissler had given Deadalus an assignment to exterminate a group of innocent artists. Deadalus, who was a captain in the Secret Police and Hissler's nephew, had balked at the inhumanity of the assignment. Hissler had threatened. And Deadalus had resigned from the agency in disgust. It was then that Deadalus had learned of the Secret Police's special retirement plan. It was the kind that left you six feet under.

Deadalus had managed to turn the tables on the agent who was sent to assassinate him and, with the help of the same group he had originally been assigned to exterminate, Deadalus had taken over one of the Secret Police's exclusive starships.

Since then Deadalus had been training them night and day, trying to form them into a crew that could man one of the most sophisticated fighting machines ever developed.

They had all been more than willing to learn, which was not too surprising. Becoming expert fighters was their only chance of staying alive.

Deadalus was satisfied that they were trained as well as they could possibly be in the time given. He was actually surprised at how well they did. But as of yet they had not faced a real test. And no matter how well you trained and prepared a man, you could never tell how he was going to react under live fire. With the high technology of the starship's weapons, there was no room for hesitation or indecision. Deadalus had no way of being certain how well the crew would do until it came down to an actual fight. One thing working to their advantage was that the weaponry of the starship was much more advanced than the weapons of any of the small local police they were likely to run into. But Deadalus didn't relish any full-fledged confrontations with another SP starship.

With any bad luck, this just might turn out to be their first test.

"How much time do you think we've got?" Whiskey asked as he adjusted the strap on his headset.

"Only a couple hours at most. The best that I could determine, the Secret Police ship was the same distance from Meer as we were. Hopefully, we made a little better time."

Deadalus took note of the young man's frown.

"We still have a distinct advantage over them, Whiskey. We're expecting them, whereas they don't know we're coming."

"I'd just as soon stay clear of them all together. I've seen enough of the Secret Police to last me the rest of my life."

There was nothing to argue in that and Deadalus changed the subject.

"What do you know about Meer?"

"Not very much. It's mostly water isn't it?"

"About 80 percent. Here, let me get the landing map."

Deadalus got the 3-D map on the display screen. The computer-generated picture of the planet turned slowly, showing the large expanse of green blue water. When a small, dark area of land came into view, Deadalus stopped the picture and had it zoom in. On closer view the land mass looked like a large island diced into a thousand pieces by a million crisscrossing rivers.

Deadalus explained that the land was actually composed of 354 separate islands, all so closely grouped that they were easily linked by a series of bridges. In a ring around these islands were miles of floating hydrofarms which, along with the fishing, produced all the food needed. Around the outer rim of the farms was a breakwater.

The entire population of the planet lived on the islands, which were completely and systematically built up with high-rise apartments and industrial buildings. Though basically self-sufficient, the planet had built up a strong export business for industrial and high-tech goods. Meer was also famous for its university, drawing specialists from all over the galaxy to teach and participate in research. It was at this university that Dr. Pablo was employed.

Deadalus put the entry pattern on the screen as they approached the planet. They called in, identifying themselves as being from a transport ship coming down to pick up supplies. They landed at the public space port, which occupied an entire island, and passed through customs without a hitch.

The black sky sparkled with unfamiliar constellations. There were still two hours of night left and Deadalus hoped that they'd be gone before dawn.

They boarded a public commuter boat. Though it was possible to get from one island to the other on foot, the quickest and most common method of transportation was by water. The commuter boat was a long and thin hydrofoil type designed especially for Meer's narrow and twisted canals.

After only a few moments of speeding along the dark, narrow canals, Whiskey realized that he was completely lost. The canal would not go straight for more than fifty yards before it would twist off in some new direction. And all the crisscrossing intersections all looked the same. When, at one of the boat's stops, Deadalus indicated that they should get off, Whiskey found that he was unable to even determine the general direction from which they had come. He usually had a very good sense of direction and so found the helpless feeling of being lost very disturbing.

Deadalus, who had been on Meer a number of times, was not quite so helpless. Though he could never say exactly where they were, he had learned the trick of getting from one point to another. He knew his way to Dr. Pablo's residence and he could only hope that that was where they were holding him. As they turned down the doctor's street, Deadalus was relieved to see two uniformed men in front of the scientist's residence.

Even in the dark and from a distance Deadalus was able to determine that the uniformed men were local police and not from the Empirical Secret Police. The two guards were, in the first place, too openly visible. And in the second place they were too relaxed.

"Looks like we got here in time, Whiskey. Just follow my lead and keep your gun on low force. We won't need any unnecessary killing."

The two policemen tensed as they saw Whiskey and Deadalus approaching them.

"And I say you don't know what you're talking about," Deadalus said in a loud, drunken voice.

The guards exchanged disgusted glances and relaxed.

"You're drunk," Whiskey bellowed back drunkenly.

"Me? Me drunk?"

They were now abreast of the doorway where the guards stood and Deadalus stopped.

"And just who was it that got us here in the first place?" Deadalus inquired increduously.

"Move along," one of the guards said gruffly.

"Whosat?" Deadalus peered in the policeman's direction, stepping closer as if to get a better view.

The two uniformed men stepped forward forcefully as if they thought the mere sight of them would scare off the two drunks.

"Move along or I'm going to run you in," the one guard repeated.

"Hey, I didn't do nothing," Deadalus whined, stepping up to the guard and taking hold of his sleeve as if trying to confidently convince him of his innocence. The guard disgustedly tried to shake off Deadalus's hand.

Whiskey, who had been watching Deadalus for the sign, choreographed his motions to coincide perfectly with his captain's. As Deadalus's hand came chopping down on the side of the one policeman's head, Whiskey's fist was simultaneously smashing into the other's larnyx. A half a moment later the two policemen lay slumped unconscious on the ground.

Deadalus glanced up and down the darkened street and then opened the door to the residence, motioning for Whiskey to help drag the two fallen men inside. Deadalus closed the door behind them and there was a moment of complete blackness until he found the switch and turned on the lights.

Deadalus was happily surprised at how smooth it had gone. With teamwork like that they could take on a whole army.

As they were tying up the policemen with their own binds, the door to the inner room slammed open.

"And what do you think you're doing?"

The man who followed in after the sharp question was tall and lean, with a fierce, scowling face adorned with white eyebrows so bushy they were kept in balance only by the bristling moustache perched belligerently beneath his sharp nose. Though he was obviously dressed for bed, he strode into the room as if he was commanding an army on the field of battle.

"You were told to wait outside," he barked, then stopped as he saw Deadalus straighten up.

"Good morning, Dr. Pablo. I hope we haven't disturbed you." Deadalus grinned.

"Hmph." The scientist snorted, looking Deadalus over. "They told me you were dead. A number of times."

"Did you believe them?"

"Only the first time."

In the light the doctor's face showed his age and the lines around his mouth and eyes indicated that he was more than just tired.

"I assume you know how dangerous it is here," Dr. Pablo said, his voice almost harsh.

Deadalus looked at him closely before replying.

"I wanted to find out what's going on. Why the guards?"

The scientist sighed wearily and sat down on a nearby chair, as if all his strength had suddenly disappeared.

"It seems that your uncle and I have a little disagreement. And, as usual, Chief

Hissler's methods of persuasion are more convincing than my own."

Deadalus pulled a chair over next to the old scientist and sat down. Whiskey stood nervously by the door, watching the street.

"Doesn't seem like you to pursue an agrument you can't win," Deadalus said.

"I've got no choice." The old man shook his head, his eyes far away, as if concentrating on a purpose only he could see.

"Why don't you tell me about it, Pablo?" Deadalus coaxed gently.

"There's nothing you can do, Deadalus. It would just get you in more trouble than you're already in."

"Doc, I can't be in any worse trouble than I am. Like you said, they can only kill me once. Why don't you tell me? What did you do to get the agency so riled with you?"

"They found out I was holding out on some information. A young snot-nosed kid at the lab stumbled on some research I was trying to cover up and he turned me in. They sent an agent out to question me and I made the mistake of trying to bluff my way through it. I stupidly assumed that they would give the benefit of the doubt to someone who's done so much work for them. Of course my bluff didn't work. They assumed that I must be selling the information on the black market and so they've put me under house arrest until I duplicate the information for them. So I go into the lab every day and make a lot of noise and come out with reams of figures. I suppose they'll eventually figure out that I'm not doing anything."

"Why don't you give them the information?"

"I can't."

The statement was sharp and final. Deadalus could sense that if he were holding a gun to the old man's head, he would get the same reply.

Whiskey glanced nervously over at Deadalus. The feeling of disquiet that had come from losing his sense of direction had continued to grow. His stomach felt tight and his feet seemed to itch in their boots. He wanted to leave as quickly as possible and he couldn't understand why the captain was just sitting there talking. If he wanted to talk to the old man, they ought to take him back to the ship, where they would all be safer. Whiskey looked back out down the dark street, watching for any sign of movement.

"What's so important about this information, Doc?"

The scientist eyed Deadalus sharply as if he momentarily suspected him of still working for the Secret Police.

"It wouldn't do you any good to know, Deadalus," he replied shaking his head.

"Listen, Pablo, I think your time's just about run out," Deadalus said almost sternly. "We picked up a message that a starship is coming here to get you and extract all the information out of you. You should know as well as I that the Secret Police have certain methods of interrogation that never fail. You're going to end up telling them anyway, so why not tell me first and maybe I can do something to help you. Now what's so vital about this information that you're willing to let them turn you into a mindless idiot to get?"

The old man's shoulders had visibly sagged under the weight of Deadalus's words. He looked shrunken, almost helpless; a completely different man than the fierce man barking commands who had entered the room a few minutes earlier.

"It's no good, Deadalus," he sighed, his voice hardly more than a hoarse whisper. "I'll kill myself before I'd let them put me under a probe. You see . . ." the old man hesitated, then, taking a deep breath, continued. "I made a breakthrough on some biological research I was doing. It was one of those types of things that could almost be called an accident. I was progressing from just a hunch, I had no real data to go on. But suddenly everything seemed to work. I had developed a genetically engineered bacteria that seemed to kill brain tumors. I was exalted, even though I wasn't sure how I was doing it. But then something strange started happening to the healthy mice that I was experimenting on. The bacteria wasn't killing them, it was doing something odd. I tried to correct it but I couldn't because I didn't really understand how the bacteria was working in the first place. Frustrated at coming so close to a monumental breakthrough just to be thwarted, I stayed away from the lab for a week and just thought. Little by little I came to understand how the bacteria worked. Finally I came to a complete understanding and realized that, instead of inventing a great medical aid for man, I had developed what was probably the most atrocious weapon that ever existed."

"I don't really see . . ." Deadalus began, but the scientist interrupted him sharply.

"What is it that keeps a tyrant from killing off the masses?"

"Because he needs them, I guess."

"Precisely. Our wonderful galactic government spends huge amounts of money and countless men to keep the conquered masses obedient. It would be much simpler to just kill them all off. But it's these same disobedient masses which give the government all its wealth. It can't kill them off because it would starve to death. Well, it turns out that this bacteria I stumbled on takes from an organism all of its willpower, but in no other way physically or mentally harms it. After being exposed to the bacteria, a person is completely able to function, *but without any will of his own*. And not only that, but the bacteria is passed on from the mother to the child through the blood."

Deadalus chewed on his lip as he digested this information. The Empire would only have to expose all the conquered planets to this bacteria and they would end up with billions of perfect slaves. *Forever.* The Empirical rulers would never have to use force, never have to compromise, everyone would do exactly as they were told without the least bit of trouble. The image of the galaxy peopled with endless generations of races without will was horrifying.

"So," the scientist continued, "when I realized what I had done, I went back to the lab and destroyed all of my research papers. They know in what area I was working and, if they really want to, they might be able to retrace some of my research. But it won't happen very soon, if ever. I had stumbled on the bacteria almost by accident. It's possible that no one, even if they were trying to, will ever duplicate it. I'm the only one who can tell them, and I'm going to make sure I don't."

"You're going to kill yourself," Deadalus said, more a statement than an actual question.

"Is there any other way?" Doctor Pablo asked wearily.

"Yes." Deadalus stood up quickly. "At least for the time being. Come with me back to my starship. We can keep you out of their hands for a while. Maybe with your help we'll be able to permanently damage their tyrannical rule. Come on, it's worth a try. And if we fail, well, you'll be in no worse spot than you are now."

The old man shook his head without even looking at Deadalus.

"I can't."

"Why not? What have you got to lose?"

"Rhea."

The softly spoken name made Deadalus's face fall and he sat back down. Rhea was Pablo's daughter. Her mother had died in childbirth and the scientist had channelled all the intensity of the emotional loss into love for his daughter. He raised her and taught her by himself, pushing his considerable skills to the utmost to make her the best possible life. Deadalus had watched the scientist put his whole heart and soul into the young girl.

"They've been threatening Rhea?" he asked.

"They've got her under guard. They've promised that as long as I comply with them, nothing will happen to her. If I were to kill myself, I don't think they would bother with her. But if I were to go with you and fight against them . . ." the old man shuddered at the thought of what the secret police would do to his daughter. "No, Deadalus, I can't risk it. Life isn't worth that much to me."

Deadalus remained quiet in thought for a few minutes. Whiskey, unable to contain his agitation, paced back and forth by the door, his attention divided between the dark street and the two men lost in conversation.

Finally Deadalus stood back up.

"I'll tell you what, Doc. How about if I get Rhea to come with us?"

The scientist looked at Deadalus with disbelief, then his eyes brightened. The life that he had given up all hope in seemed suddenly renewed.

"What are we waiting for?" he barked, shooting erect to his feet. "Let's get going." His face was once again filled with the fierce commanding look it had when they'd first come in.

"Alright, this is the way we'll do it," Deadalus motioned Whiskey over. "There's no sense in the three of us running around in this watery maze. Too much chance of getting spotted. Doc, you go with Whiskey back to our landing craft at the space port. I'll go get Rhea and meet you there. Where are they keeping Rhea?"

The scientist frowned doubtfully at Deadalus.

"They just have her under house arrest over at the university. But I think I should come with you. You might need some help or something."

"No. I can move much faster by myself. And I think I can handle them, thank you. Now why don't you give me directions? And you'd best make them explicit."

Pablo gave him the address and directions.

"Now don't do anything to get her hurt," the old man cautioned. "If there's any chance at all that she might get hurt, I want you to just forget it."

"I won't let her get hurt," Deadalus assured.

The scientist eyed Deadalus skeptically and then seemed to decide to accept his assurance and went quickly into the other room to get ready.

Deadalus waited until Pablo had left the

room, then he turned to Whiskey and spoke in a low voice.

"I don't want you to take any risks at all, Whiskey. Dr. Pablo is too important. You just get to the landing craft and keep your eyes open. If you see anything at all that looks like trouble, you take off. Understand?"

The younger man nodded. "How long should I wait for you?"

Deadalus glanced at his watch.

"Give me two hours. If we don't get there by then, chances are we aren't coming. Don't wait any longer than that because it'll be starting to get light. OK?"

Deadalus smiled and slapped the frowning Whiskey playfully on the shoulder.

"Cheer up, Whiskey. I'll stop off at a store and pick us up some brandy on my way back."

Deadalus opened the door, glanced quickly up and down the street, and then disappeared into the darkness.

Whiskey nervously watched him leave and then closed the door. His feeling of uneasiness kept growing. It seemed to him that too much time had been wasted in talking. They were lucky to have gotten here before the Secret Police as it was. It didn't make any sense to sit around and wait for them to catch up.

He went over and checked on the two policemen, who were still lying bound on the floor. They were out, but he couldn't tell for how long. Whiskey set his gun on the lowest setting and gave each of the men a jolt.

The gun was a specially designed Secret Police weapon which emitted a low level electrically charged laser beam. The gun had a number of unique characteristics, one of which was that the extent of the injury could be controlled from mere pain all the way up to instant death. The weapon left no mark on the victim except at point-blank range, in which case it left a third-degree burn the size of a finger ring. Otherwise, death by an electrically charged laser was indistinguishable from a heart attack. It was a fairly new kind of handgun and the only people who were supposed to have them were the agents of the Empirical Secret Police. It was one of the weapons on board the *Orpheus* when they had stolen the starship from the Secret Police.

Whiskey gave the two policemen enough of a jolt to keep them unconscious for three or four hours.

Whiskey paced anxiously back and forth for a few minutes and then finally went in to see what was taking so long. The doctor was gathering together a few personal belongings, putting them in a small luggage bag. Whiskey hurried him up as much as he could, but it still took an exasperating ten minutes before the scientist was ready.

Much later, Whiskey was to concede that the fact that he had that bag in his hand and not his gun as they stepped out into the street probably saved his life.

As he was closing the door behind them, Whiskey caught a movement out of the corner of his eye. He whirled, but never got the chance to complete the motion.

Something crashed against the back of his skull and the black night turned red.

chapter two

Deadalus looked at his watch. Twenty-five minutes had elapsed since he had left the doctor's house. He looked out the port-side window of the transport boat he was on. The buildings that lined the shore of the canals seemed hardly more than an arm's reach away as they sped by in the near blackness.

It must be the boat pilot's last run for the night. He steered the nearly empty public boat through the canals at an unbelievable speed, making only the briefest stops.

The few other people on the boat were all of the type seen on nearly any other planet at this time of night. The handful of unshaven derelicts either snoring in a drunken sleep or looking through the pockets of their coats for something even they are uncertain of. There were the two sturdy-looking workers who were either coming home from the night shift or on their way to the early-morning shift. And then over in the corner the lady who, though not old, had that worn and tired look of someone who was never young.

Glancing at the other passengers, Deadalus almost felt like he had seen each of them many times before, so often had he found himself out in this odd late-night hour. He turned back and looked out the window, carefully keeping track of the signs and landmarks. He didn't want to miss his stop. If he got lost now, it could easily be hours before he'd find his way back again.

They came to his stop at the university and Deadalus disembarked, standing back from the splash as the hydrofoil boat sped off. He looked around, going over in his mind the directions that Dr. Pablo had given him.

The living area for the students was on a small island next to the island which he was on. Deadalus was sure that he would recognize it, remembering having seen once before the huge, flat, featureless high rises that housed the university's hundreds of thousands of students.

He started off on the road next to the canal, attentively watching the road and waterway for police. The last thing he wanted was to be stopped and questioned, even in a routine manner.

Deadalus tried to recall what he knew

about Rhea. If she was attending the university, she must be a lot older than he remembered. Seemed like the last time he saw her she was just a giggling little girl. But when he counted back the years, he was surprised to realize that she must be over twenty.

She'd always been bright. Having one of the galaxy's greatest scientists as teacher, father, and constant companion, she couldn't help but be. But now she was going to be in a lot of trouble unless Deadalus could get her in time.

Deadalus found the building Pablo had directed him to. There was no one about on the street. Rhea's apartment was on the twenty-first floor. Deadalus took the primitive electromagnetic lift up, drawing his gun as he reached her level. He checked the corridor. It was empty. There wasn't even a guard outside her door.

Deadalus stopped and thought. Something wasn't right. Perhaps they had moved her. It would be impossible for Deadalus to find her by himself if they had. And it didn't seem likely that they would just leave her unattended.

He checked his gun to make sure it was still on low power, then he looked over the apartment door. It was locked, but the mechanism was not very sophisticated and would not prove much trouble. Deadalus wished he could know what was on the other side of the door before he opened it, but there was no way to see into the apartment.

Forcing the lock, Deadalus opened the door a crack and peered in. The room inside was dim. Seeing no one, he opened the door, slipped in, and closed the door silently behind him.

There was a light coming in from a doorway on his left, and, as he listened, he could make out the sounds of voices and movements. He crept over to the doorway and looked in.

A large piece of furniture was partially blocking Deadalus's view and at first he couldn't make out what was going on. There were two or three uniformed policemen bunched together over at the other side of the room, holding something on the floor. The torn, discarded nightgown and the bare feminine legs gave Deadalus a clue as to what that something was.

Still crouching, Deadalus thumbed his gun up to full power and slowly moved along the wall, trying to get a clear shot. There wasn't going to be any room for an awkward aim.

The three guards were so intent on what they were doing that they didn't notice Deadalus. Two of them were holding Rhea's arms pinned to the floor while the third, his pants down around his ankles, was on top of the naked girl.

The one who was raping her was thrusting with such violence that he would have impelled her across the floor had not the other two been restraining her. Deadalus could hear the man swearing under his heavy breath, warning Rhea not to scream. But the girl, with her eyes shut, had her teeth clenched tight, as if intent on denying him at least the one pleasure of hearing her agony.

Deadalus scuttled over behind a chair, took careful aim, and fired. Because his gun was a magnetic-field-laser type and could, at full power, cut through a number of people at the same time, Deadalus had to be careful not to hit Rhea at the same time that he was shooting the man on top of her. His marksmanship being what it was, Deadalus's shot burned a neat hole clear through the top of the guard's head. A blink of an eye later there was a geyser of bright red blood spurting a foot and a half into the air.

One of the other policemen leaped to his feet in confusion and looked wildly about the room as if trying to find a place to hide. Before he could take a single step, Deadalus's laser raked across him, slicing him neatly in half and leaving a smoldering scar on the wall behind him.

The third policeman was still crouching, but just as Deadalus swung his gun around to fire, Rhea sat up screaming and threw the dead policeman off her. Deadalus held his fire and the guard, seeing his chance, drew his gun with one hand and grabbed Rhea around the neck with his other arm.

"Drop your gun or I'll kill her!" the policeman yelled, choking the girl so hard her face started to turn purple.

Deadalus knew that the demand was ridiculous, because if the policeman killed Rhea he would have nothing to protect himself with. But as long as he kept her between himself and Deadalus, Deadalus couldn't shoot.

Sensing this, the policeman desperately dragged Rhea to her feet and fired two shots vaguely in Deadalus's direction. His gun, which used soft bullets, was only dangerous with direct hits. But the guard's shots were so wild they didn't even hit the chair that Deadalus was crouched behind.

Deadalus watched helplessly as the guard, still choking Rhea so hard she couldn't breathe, backed slowly toward the door.

chapter three

It felt like someone had been using his head for target practice. Someone with exceptionally good aim.

Slowly, Whiskey became aware that not all the roaring in his ears was coming from his pounding brain. Ache by ache, his senses began functioning. The roaring, he now realized, was definitely coming from the cold surface that his head was pressed against. Struggling, he cracked open one eye.

A boot, huge, scuffed, and stained, presented itself a few inches from the end of his nose. Whiskey closed his eye on the rather unpleasant sight and tried to think.

The strange, bouncing sensation was familiar. It was the distinct motion of a hydrofoil boat. That would account for the roaring as well. And the sharp pain in his wrist was probably caused by plastic handcuffs cutting into his skin because of the awkward way he was lying.

So much for where he was. As to how he got there, the man wearing the boot could probably be thanked for that. The style of footwear was unmistakable. It was the same as his own. It was Empirical Police issue.

Whiskey didn't even bother trying to figure out what was going to happen next. It was obvious he didn't have any choice but to wait and see.

They came to a stop and there was the shuffling of feet. Whiskey felt himself being lifted up and carried out of the boat. He opened his eyes just in time to catch a brief glimpse of the colored flashing lights, which could only be the spaceport, and then he was dumped unceremoniously into some kind of cargo trolley.

In the dim light that came down over the high sides of the trolley car, Whiskey could see that Dr. Pablo was lying on the floor next to him, similarily bound and still unconscious. Whiskey struggled to a sitting position in the cramped space.

Though the situation couldn't really get any worse, it didn't seem to be improving much either. His only hope was that Deadalus could stay free long enough to bring some help. As far as Whiskey knew, his captors had no idea who he was and he hoped to keep it that way. They wouldn't be too gracious if they found that he was a crew member of the starship *Orpheus*.

Like nearly everyone else in the galaxy, Whiskey had heard vague and horrifying rumors about the Secret Police's methods for getting people to divulge information. It was said that they had methods which were guaranteed to work, though some of them left you more dead than alive. Whiskey wasn't certain how much of what he'd heard was true. And he certainly hoped that he wouldn't find out. He was going to have to come up with some kind of believable story.

"Hey, Bull, this one's come around," a voice in the night said as the trolley came to a stop and the side was lowered.

"Must not have hit him hard enough," another voice muttered back. "Least I won't have to carry him."

Whiskey was hoisted to his feet and, with his head spinning, was led up a ship ramp. Through half-shut eyes he managed to make out the shape of a landing craft a good deal bigger than the *Ezra*, the *Orpheus*'s landing craft in which they had arrived.

Inside, Whiskey was taken into a room which looked like a sickbay and pushed down into a seat. He was strapped down by the one who had been called Bull, while the other agent, Dr. Pablo draped over his shoulder, went to another part of the ship.

Bull was no doubt the ugliest man Whiskey had ever seen. He had a broad, flat face, accented by eyes which were so extremely small and close set they were kept apart only by the intrusion of a smashed, upturned nose. But the most dominant feature on his whole grotesque face was a hideous harelip. The raw gash which split the lip clear up to the base of the nose was so wide that a quarter inch of yellowed teeth showed through even when his mouth was closed.

The agent caught Whiskey staring at his face and, almost as if by accident, jabbed his thumb in the young man's eye.

"Keep staring at me and you're going to end up just as ugly," he muttered.

Firmly strapped in the seat and with his hands bound behind his back, Whiskey didn't consider himself in much of a position to express his disagreement. So he remained silent, glaring at Bull painfully out of his one good eye. His anger helped to clear his head. If he needed a purpose for staying alive, he now had one. He had to survive so that he could revenge himself on Bull.

"Hey, Dirk, what did Captain Webern say?" Bull asked as the other agent came into the cabin.

"He says we're to get this guy's story while we wait."

"Wait for what?"

"They went to pick up the old man's daughter. Going to use her on him, I guess."

"Oh yeah? Sure hope I get to do the using," Bull's chuckle sounded more like a dying animal than an indication of humor.

Whiskey listened carefully to their conversation, trying to pick up any word of Deadalus.

"I bet you would," Dirk laughed. "She's supposed to be just your type. One of those intellectuals."

"Oh, I love intellectual young ladies."

The two agents laughed together as if at some private joke and the sound was enough to make Whiskey shudder.

"What are we supposed to get from this?" Bull asked, indicating Whiskey. "We already know all he has to say."

"Procedures, Bull. Got to follow procedures."

"He don't look like the cooperative type."

The two agents stood looking down on Whiskey, Bull's face in a continual snarl and Dirk looking somewhat bored.

"You want to just tell us who you are and what you were doing?" the latter asked. "Save Bull the trouble of twisting it out of you. Though confidentially, mister, I must admit that it's more pleasure than chore for Bull here."

Whiskey looked back and forth between the two agents, then, calculatingly licked his lip, hesitating.

"I . . . I don't know what's going on. I was just visiting the doctor, I'm a friend of his and . . ."

With one thick hand Bull grabbed Whiskey around the throat, choking off Whiskey's proffered explanation. Forcing Whiskey's head back, Bull jabbed a dirty thumbnail in the taut-stretched skin under Whiskey's jaw, painfully drawing blood.

The physical pain was nowhere near as shocking as the almost obscene nonchalance of the gesture. Bull might have been pulling the wings off a fly, so little emotion did he show. And Whiskey realized that his life meant as little to Bull as that fly's.

"Alright," he gasped when Bull let go of his throat. "Alright. I don't really know the guy. A friend of a friend put me in contact with him. He was going to pay me to smuggle him off of Meer."

"Is that right," Dirk yawned, leaning against one of the metal cabinets. "And just where is it that you were supposed to be taking him?"

Whiskey tried to think of the most preposterous thing he could.

"Earth."

"What?" Dirk laughed and Bull grunted in disgust.

"I really don't know nothing about it," Whiskey spoke quickly. "That's what he wanted, and he offered to pay pretty good. So I was going to oblige him. I don't know what kind of trouble he was in. I didn't ask. I'm just a small-time trader. Been having pretty hard times lately. I've never done nothing like this before. Listen guys, I got a wife and kid to feed. I don't like doing this sort of thing, but he was offering good money and it didn't seem that big of a deal. What do you want me to do?"

Whiskey watched the two agents carefully. He didn't expect them to believe the story. In fact, he was counting on them to disbelieve it. From what he had heard at the doctor's apartment and here, he gathered that they thought that he was working in the black market. The punishment for being a marketeer, as they were called, was pretty severe. But Whiskey would gladly suffer it if it meant that they wouldn't find out that he was from the *Orpheus*. The punishment for that, he was sure, would be much worse.

So Whiskey was trying to do his best to appear as a marketeer. If he came right out and claimed to be in illegal trading, they were sure to get suspicious. So he offered them another story so that they would have to force out of him the information they expected to hear. That way his final story would be all the more believable.

The two agents glanced at each other and then Dirk sighed and shook his head.

"I'm really disappointed in you. I thought for sure you'd be a quick learner." He nodded wearily to Bull, who just grinned and advanced toward Whiskey.

"Hey listen! I'm telling you the truth!" Whiskey managed to squeak out in a panicky voice before Bull's thick fist came crashing down across his jaw.

His head spun from the blow and for a minute he thought that he might fall into unconsciousness again. But he shook his head, fighting it off. When his sight had once again cleared, the two guards were still watching him; Dirk obviously bored and Bull with his harelip pronounced by a hideous grin.

"Let me be a little more explicit," Dirk said. "We already know you're a marketeer. In fact, we know just about all there is to know about you. We just have to get you to admit to it as a matter of procedure. So why not save us time and yourself some unnecessary pain, and tell us?"

Whiskey hesitated a moment, looking at Bull. Then, taking a deep breath he shook his head.

"I don't know what you're talking about," he replied between gritted teeth, and waited for the blow to fall.

This time the Secret Police agent displayed a bit more expertise, jabbing two thick fingers between Whiskey's ribs in a motion nearly too fast for the eye to follow.

Instantly the young man's breath was knocked out and a paralyzing pain shot up his left side.

It took a minute for Whiskey's breathing apparatus to begin functioning enough for him to vocalize his pain, which he did without restraint. Much to Bull's obvious pleasure.

Dirk came over and put his hand on Whiskey's shoulder, leaning over and speaking to him in a confidential tone.

"It's just going to get more and more painful. You know you aren't going to hold out too much longer. Now don't you think it would be much easier to just answer our questions?"

Whiskey nodded.

"Why don't we start with the simple ones. Like, what's your name?"

Without hesitation Whiskey gave them the name which was on the passport papers he'd used to get on Meer.

"Sam Pepper. But you already know that," he muttered as if reluctantly.

"There's not much we don't already know," Dirk snapped back. "You just worry about giving us straight answers and I'll worry about the questions. Where are you from?"

"I was born on Krnton, in the H-3 sector, if that's what you mean. Haven't been there in years though."

"What's your occupation?"

"I'm a navigator on a trader."

"What do you trade in?"

"Anything people want to buy. Listen, if you know all this why . . ." Whiskey let the question go unfinished as Bull raised his fist, reading a reply.

"What's the name of your ship?" Dirk asked in a bored voice.

"The *Dandelion*." Whiskey risked a glance around the cabin. The conversation was obviously being recorded or the agents wouldn't be going through such worthless formalities, but he was unable to spot where the recording device was. Not that it made any difference.

"What was your business with Dr. Pablo?"

"He was selling us some kind of information."

"What kind?"

"I don't know."

A sudden blow to his solar plexus knocked his breath out.

"What kind of information?" Dirk repeated.

"I don't know! The captain doesn't confide in me! If every crew member on the ship knew all that the captain does, they'd soon find no need for the captain. All I know is that he was selling us some kind of information."

"Who's your captain?"

Before Whiskey could answer this question, the cabin door slid open and Whiskey knew by the alert reaction of the two agents even before he saw his insignia that this was the captain of the Secret Police ship.

Captain Webern was fairly tall and looked to be in his late thirties. He moved with an easy grace that indicated a combination of extreme physical fitness and personal confidence. Though his face was stern it was not hard, and his eyes held the glimmer of a strong intelligence. Whiskey met his gaze for a moment then looked away. It was apparent even at first glance that the captain wasn't in the same class as the two agents. He was a man as highly skilled and trained as Deadalus. The thought made Whiskey suddenly lose hope in his story.

"Who is the captain of the *Dandelion*?"

Dirk repeated, his voice much crisper than before the captain had entered.

"Buckwell. Captain Buckwell. Least that's what he calls himself."

As Whiskey answered, he watched out of the corner of his eye as the Secret Police captain sat down on the table next to the possessions which had been removed from Whiskey at the time of his capture.

"How long have you been serving on the *Dandelion*?" Dirk continued the questioning.

" 'Bout two years. Had my own ship before that. An old clunker by the name of *Clyde*. An old prewar ferry, of the Future-Four type. Made my living salvaging. Wasn't too bad of a living either. Until the Empire taxed me out of it."

"Where were you selling the information?"

"What?" Whiskey, who had been telling the story for the captain's benefit, had lost track of what Dirk was asking.

"Where were you trying to sell the information you got from Dr. Pablo?"

"I don't know. Told you before, the captain don't tell me all his secrets. Heard talk about some representative of some chemical manufacturer."

"Where were you taking the doctor when we caught you?"

"Here."

"Here?"

"The spaceport I mean." Whiskey silently cursed himself for the slip. He didn't want

37

them to start suspecting him of being too observant.

"And what were you to do after you brought him to the spaceport?" Dirk continued, evidently not noticing the break in Whiskey's character.

"We were supposed to be met here."

While Whiskey was being questioned, Captain Webern had been looking intently through his belongings, which were piled next to him on the table. Whiskey felt a slow chill start creeping up his spine as he saw the captain pick up his gun off the table and start twirling it around his finger as if lost in thought.

"I'll tell you something, though," Whiskey said somewhat nervously. "I can guarantee you that the captain would never have touched that Pablo character if he'd a' known that you guys were involved. We thought he was just in trouble with the locals. We would have stayed good and clear if we knew you Empirical Police were after him."

The Secret Police captain was making Whiskey extremely nervous and the young man wished that the agent would finish with his questioning.

"What kind of ship is the *Dandelion*?"

"Uh, it's a class Four-A, Seafin type with solid fuel bosters. It has an acceleration of eighteen free-fall G's and . . ."

"We're familiar with the type," Dirk waved Whiskey silent as he was about to give a detailed description of the most common small-ship design in the galaxy.

"Well, captain," Dirk said, turning to his superior. "It's pretty much just as we thought."

Captain Webern looked at Dirk with a small smile.

"Isn't that surprising," he said softly.

"Beg your pardon, sir?"

The captain didn't answer and Dirk glanced uneasily over at Bull. Finding no kind of help there, he continued.

"What do you want us to do with him now, sir? We could just turn him over to the locals, they're pretty strict with marketeers in this sector."

"Marketeers?" The captain looked at Dirk quizzically.

"Yes, sir. The man here . . . that is . . ." Dirk stopped, confused.

The captain turned and looked at Whiskey, who met his gaze for a moment and then looked down at the floor.

"So you're a black marketeer are you?" the captain asked.

Whiskey sighed, then nodded.

"And you had no idea that you'd be running afoul of the Empirical Secret Police, did you?"

"No. Never would have gotten involved if we knew there was any chance of that."

"Hmm. Yes. Black marketeers seem to stay pretty clear of us, don't they?"

As the captain was looking at Dirk when he said this, the agent gulped and nodded uncertainly.

Captain Webern stood up, still tossing

Whiskey's gun in his hand, and walked over to the bound young man.

"Mind telling me where you got this gun?" he asked, pointing the weapon at Whiskey.

Whiskey glanced at the gun but didn't raise his eyes to meet the captain's.

"Captain Buckwell gave it to me."

"Is that right? This gun happens to be an exclusive weapon of the Empirical Secret Police. No marketeer would ever touch it."

"How am I supposed to know where . . ."

"You happen to know what an edge-jumper is?" the captain asked before Whiskey could finish.

"No," he replied sullenly, the chill starting to spread.

"How about a cal-scan? Do you know what a cal-scan is?"

"Listen, I told you everything I know."

"The only problem is that you seem to know too little," Captain Webern said harshly. "Any marketeer would know what an edge-jumper and a cal-scan are. Any marketeer would know that this was a Secret Police weapon."

Whiskey looked down at the floor, bitterly aware that his whole cover story had just collapsed.

"You're not a marketeer. Now why don't you tell us who you really are and what you're after."

Whiskey remained silent.

Bull reached over to hit him but Captain Webern stopped him.

"Don't waste your time. You'll get nothing out of him like that."

"What's his game, captain?" Dirk asked.

Webern's jaw was set and his eyes were blazing. "I'll give you a hint," he replied softly. "The man would obviously be happy to suffer the fate of a marketeer rather than be found out for what he really is."

The captain let the idea sink in, then turned briskly and started for the door.

"You two keep him under guard. I'll get back to you." He stopped and looked at Bull. "And I don't want him damaged. He's got a lot of talking still to do."

When Captain Webern left the cabin where they were holding Whiskey he went directly to the bridge of the ship and sat down in front of the main computer terminal. He punched in a request to be connected with the central information bank of the Empirical government. He sat back frowning while he waited for the hookup to be completed.

He had a pretty good idea of what it was that the prisoner was trying to hide. It was the weapon which had tipped him off. There just weren't very many of those guns around. And then, listening to the prisoner talk, he realized how adroitly his agents were being misled. Sure Dirk and Bull weren't exactly the brightest agents on the force, but they were fully trained and had been around enough to know most of the tricks. But the young man had pulled off the story so well that, Webern realized, he himself might have been taken in if it weren't for the gun. The prisoner seemed to have been trained by someone who was an expert in deceit. And all the experts in that field worked for the Secret Police. That is, all but one of them.

When the terminal indicated that the hook-up was completed, Captain Webern quickly punched in his request for all available information concerning Captain Deadalus and his band of outlaws.

It didn't take very long for Webern to confirm his suspicions. Under the listing of persons known or believed to be working with Deadalus, the first one pictured was his prisoner, Winchester Milton—Whiskey.

The captain studied the information and then turned the terminal off. He sat back, rubbing his chin and thinking. Then, nervously straightening his uniform and brushing back his hair, he put through a call to Chief Hissler.

After giving all the proper codes and indentifications, Webern was finally connected with the chief.

Hissler's face, which now filled the screen, was as hideous as Bull's but in a completely different manner. Whereas Bull gave one the feeling of some kind of horrendous bug which should be immediately squashed, Hissler's ugliness was more a matter of character than actual physical appearance. It was the type of ugliness that gave form to all the evilness in one's nightmares. It was a terrifying rather than merely repulsive ugliness.

Hissler's nose was long and sharp, jutting out like the beak of some predatory bird. His mouth was so thin and usually drawn so tight in perpetual displeasure that it nearly disappeared altogether. His eyes were as sharp as two laser beams. If lasers could be as black as night.

"What's the problem, Webern?" The chief snapped before the captain even had time to say anything. "You have any problem getting Pablo?"

"Uh, no sir, no problem there."

"Did you get the information out of him?"

"We haven't questioned him yet, sir. I wanted to report on another development. While picking up Dr. Pablo, we also apprehended another man whom I believe to be Winchester Milton. A man known to be one of Deadalus's crew members."

Hissler's face suddenly came alive. The corner of his mouth started twitching and his brows narrowed with intensity.

"You have him? Alive?"

"Yes, sir. We caught him along with the doctor. He had overcome the two local policemen who were guarding Pablo and was just leaving when we apprehended him."

"With the doctor? What was he doing there?"

"He hasn't said," Webern replied, then added, "yet."

But the chief didn't seem to be listening.

"Deadalus and the starship must be somewhere in the area," Hissler was saying excitedly. "This is the best break we've had yet. We'll get that bastard this time."

"Yes sir."

"Any chance that Deadalus knows you're on to him?"

"I've no idea, sir. As I said, the prisoner's not yet talked."

"Well, you're going to have to rectify that, aren't you, Captain?" Hissler snapped.

"Yes, sir."

"I want you to put him under the probe and get everything you can out of him. I'm going to put out a general alert and get everything available over to your area. I'll see if the military has anything in that sector that we can use."

"What about the doctor?"

"Pablo? You think he's tied in with this?"

"Well, sir, the prisoner was with him when we took them into custody."

Chief Hissler's face furrowed in concentrated thought.

"What would Deadalus want with Pablo, I wonder," he muttered, more to himself than to the captain. "Listen, Webern, my guess is that Pablo doesn't really have anything to do with Deadalus. But on the off chance that he might know something, put him under the probe as well."

"The doctor, sir?" Captain Webern asked somewhat incredulously.

"That's what I said, damnit."

"Dr. Pablo is, uh, rather old sir. I couldn't guarantee that he would survive a session under the probe—sir," Webern added hesitantly.

"Who asked you for any goddamned guarantees!" Hissler bellowed back.

"Yes, sir, I only meant, sir, what about the other information I was supposed to get from the doctor, sir?" the captain said quickly.

"Get that too, of course. But that's not the important thing right now. Deadalus is the most important. I want any information Pablo has that can help us get Deadalus. That other stuff ..." Hissler frowned for a moment then waved his hand as if trying to drive off an annoying fly. "Get the other information too, but don't worry about it. Just capsulize it and we'll give it to the lab boys when you get back. Right now I'm after Deadalus and I want any information Pablo has. And I don't want you to be deterred by any sentimental considerations for his age either."

"No, sir, I only meant ..."

"The doctor has become expendable."

"Yes, sir. And what do you want me to do with the other prisoner after I probe him, sir?"

"What do you mean?"

"He may still be alive, sir."

"That's not likely enough to even worry about." Chief Hissler raised his hand as if to dismiss the captain.

"But they can survive, sir," Webern persisted. "When used properly, the probe doesn't always kill the subjects."

Hissler looked annoyed, but Webern wasn't going to back down. If the chief wanted him to kill the prisoner, he was going to have to order him to do so. If something fouled up and Deadalus got away, Captain Webern didn't want to end up being the scapegoat.

"*If* the prisoner lives through questioning," Hissler finally said, his face clearly showing his disgust, "then bring him back with you. He may have some use. Any more questions, captain?"

"Uh, no, sir."

"Good. I'll put out the general alert then and have the other ships report directly to you."

The screen abruptly went blank as the chief finished the conversation.

When the captain came back into the cabin, Whiskey was having a glaring contest with Bull, who was having trouble following the Captain's last order about leaving Whiskey undamaged. Whiskey was trying to goad the agent into losing his temper. He figured that if Bull got mad and knocked his head off, it would probably be much cleaner than whatever it was the captain had in mind.

But Bull had managed to keep himself under control, and when the captain came back in, Whiskey was still undamaged.

Captain Webern walked over and stood in

front of Whiskey. He looked at him for a long moment before he spoke.

"Alright, Whiskey, I'm not going to play games with you. I know who you are. I know you're with Deadalus. Now you can either talk freely or we'll make you talk. And believe me, it won't be pleasant if we have to make you. So how about it?"

Whiskey just looked at him without replying.

"Alright Dirk, go get the probe."

Bull grunted in surprise and Dirk looked startled.

"The probe, sir?"

"That's right, damnit. The probe."

chapter four

Deadalus felt the muscle in his calf begin to knot. He ducked another volley of shots.

The policeman backed toward the door. His arm clamped around Rhea's neck, dragging her with him.

Clawing at his arm, the naked, blood-spattered girl fought desperately for air. Her face was blue and veins stood out on the side of her head.

Deadalus shifted his weight, easing the pressure on his leg. Rhea would be unconscious in half a minute. Dead from strangulation a minute after that.

Deadalus held his gun level. Gritting his teeth, he prayed for an opening, any opening. He needed a clear shot. He couldn't risk hitting Rhea while trying to shoot the policeman. Of course, in ninety seconds that wouldn't matter.

Just at the moment that the policeman turned slightly in order to negotiate the doorway, Rhea gave up prying at his arm and, in a last desperate attempt, turned her attack to the man's ribs. Her jabbing elbow caught him by surprise. His grip loosened just enough for Rhea to break free.

Deadalus had his gun aimed but could not shoot, as Rhea was still directly in his line of fire.

The policeman made a grab for Rhea, trying to catch her again before she could run away. Deadalus leaped to his feet, intent on using Rhea's momentary distraction to his advantage.

But Rhea surprised them both. She had no intention of running away. Instead, she whirled and furiously swung both of her fists at the policeman's face.

Taken completely by surprise and, with his own forward momentum adding to the force of the blows, the policeman stumbled back, giving Deadalus, for one brief moment, a clear shot.

That moment was all Deadalus needed. He pulled the trigger on his gun and burned a fist-size hole halfway through the man's stomach.

The man fell down and Rhea leapt on him, hitting him as hard as she could, not realizing that he was dead. She was intently trying to gouge out his eyes when Deadalus finally pulled her off.

Rhea glared furiously at Deadalus, not recognizing him.

"Rhea, it's me, Deadalus." He shook her gently.

She started at the name and her glare was replaced by a look of surprised recognition.

She started to say something, but the trembling in her jaw was too great and she clamped her teeth, fighting against the tears. Her face showed the intensity of the struggle.

For the moment the tears won. Rhea broke down, sobbing. Deadalus tried to hold her, to comfort her, but she pushed him away. Shaking her head, she stepped back away from him and fought with the emotions by herself.

Deadalus could do nothing but watch her, impressed by her will and determination. Her fierce determination was reminiscent of her father.

Rhea was of average height and had shoulder-length dark brown hair, which was now, Deadalus could see, tangled and matted with blood. Though her small breasts were heaving now with the force of her sobs, he noticed that she had not been overcome by the recent exertion. The rest of her body also gave indication of her physical fitness.

Deadalus's keen powers of observation also apprised him of a number of other changes in her form since the last time he had seen her. Changes which, in another time and place, he might have felt uncomfortable in noticing. But watching her as she stood naked in the ankle-deep gore, her body covered with clots of blood, Deadalus had the uneasy feeling that they weren't out of danger yet.

With her eyes shut tight and her hands pressed against her temples, Rhea managed to overcome the tears and slowly get control of herself. When she finally seemed calm enough, she opened her eyes.

But the first glance at the blood and intestines which covered her apartment floor sent her reeling and, with her hand clapped over her mouth, she dashed into the bathroom, where she promptly got sick.

When Deadalus followed her in, she was sitting back on her heels, wiping off her face with a wet cloth. She laughed a bit uneasily.

"I don't suppose that this is much of a way to greet my knight in shining armor. But I'm awfully glad you came when you did."

"Better get cleaned up, Rhea. We've got to go."

Rhea stood up obediently and started running some water in the sink.

"What's going on, Deadalus? What are you doing here? The police mentioned that the Secret Police were coming, but I don't think they meant you."

Deadalus's sense of urgency increased with Rhea's information about the Secret Police. They'd have to hurry if they didn't want to get in trouble. He moved over to where he could keep an eye on the front door of the apartment while he tried to answer some of Rhea's questions.

"Did your father tell you about what's going on?"

"No. You know Father! He never wants to tell me anything. Always trying to protect me. I gathered he was in some kind of trouble with the chief. But I didn't know you were involved."

As she talked, Rhea soaked a number of towels and used them to wash the blood from off her breasts and thighs.

"I wasn't involved. Until tonight, that is. I can't explain it all right now, but your father is in very big trouble. I got word of it and came to see if I couldn't be of some help."

Deadalus briefly outlined the situation for her. Rhea suddenly stopped washing herself and looked at him wide-eyed.

"But the Secret Police are already on their way here!"

"So you said. How do you know?"

"That's why those . . ." she glanced toward the carnage in the other room. "They've been threatening to rape me ever since this began, in just a teasing sort of way. Then tonight they found out that they were supposed to hand me over to the Empirical Police." She stopped. "We'd better run, Deadalus."

He agreed.

She grabbed some clothes and threw them on as fast as she could, hurriedly pulling a knit cap down over her head. As he watched her dress, Deadalus realized that not all the blood she had washed off had belonged to the policemen. Her thighs were glistening red with her own blood.

Deadalus looked away at the mess which covered the apartment floor. It sure was a sloppy way to do work. He hated doing things in this manner. He hated being rushed when he didn't have everything planned out. It was in situations like these that simple chances and coincidences could get you killed. And Deadalus didn't much like to have his life dependent on coincidence.

It only took her a couple of minutes to get ready and, without the slightest hesitation at leaving all her possessions behind, she followed Deadalus to the door.

Deadalus checked the charge on his gun, felt the clips inside his tunic which held the explosives, and then carefully opened the door.

The hall was empty and silent. They started toward the lift that Deadalus had come up in, but as they got closer, Deadalus noticed that it was in use.

He put his hand out and stopped Rhea. It could be nothing. Could just be some innocent student who happened to keep odd hours. But this was no time to take chances.

"Is there another way down?"

"Sure. There's a lot of lifts at the other end of the building. And there's the emergency drop."

Deadalus turned and they headed in the

other direction. They had just about reached
the corner of the hall when he heard the lift
behind them come to a stop and the door
open. He pushed Rhea ahead of him and
glanced over his shoulder.

Two men stepped out of the lift. They were
definitely not students.

Deadalus and Rhea got around the corner
just as the agents saw them and gave a yell.
Deadalus grabbed the girl's hand and started
running.

Deadalus thought quickly, basing his plan
on what he knew about Secret Police training and methods. He let go of Rhea's hand
when he found that she could easily keep
pace with him.

The building was huge and there were
many intersecting hallways, but Deadalus
kept in a straight line until the two agents
had rounded the corner behind them. He
wanted to make sure that they were seen
and the agents knew in which direction they
were heading.

There was a shout and a laser scarred the
wall next to Deadalus's head.

Deadalus immediately pulled Rhea down
a hallway to the right and then yanked her
to a halt in the shelter of a doorway.

It didn't give them very much cover, but it
wouldn't need to if Deadalus's reasoning was
correct. His maneuver depended on the two
agents thinking that they were going to keep
running. If they did what he would do if he
was in their position, they would immedi-

ately split up, one agent following the way they'd just come, the other turning off to the right, hoping to cut them off.

Deadalus glanced down the hallway. There was another intersection about twenty yards down. That was the limit of how much time they'd have to pull this off.

He glanced down and met Rhea's gaze as she silently watched him, unable to know what he was planning and having to blindly put her trust in his ability.

Deadalus held his breath.

He could hear the soft sound of running feet as they approached across the carpeted floor. Then one of the agents came running full speed around the corner, his eyes searching the hallway in front of him, not expecting anything to come at him from the side.

There was only a portion of a second before he saw Deadalus. But by then it was too late.

Deadalus's shot killed the man instantly. Deadalus was out, catching hold of the agent even before he hit the ground. He glanced quickly back around the corner and saw the hallway was clear, then, quickly motioning Rhea to follow him, he dragged the dead agent back around the corner from the way they had come.

Just as they got safely back around the corner, Deadalus heard the other agent run into the hallway they had just left. Now just as long as the agent continued to act predictably, there wouldn't be any trouble.

Deadalus let the dead agent fall to the floor and, pushing Rhea ahead of him, began running back along the hallway toward Rhea's room. It would only take a few minutes before the agent would figure out that he was going in the wrong direction. They had to make the most of that time.

They ran past Rhea's room and got in the lift and started down.

"You alright?" he asked Rhea.

She nodded.

Deadalus didn't want to take the lift all the way to the ground floor. He had no way of knowing how many agents had come. It was very possible there would be a third or even a fourth waiting on the street level. He stopped the lift on the second floor, checked the hallway, and then had Rhea lead the way to the stairs.

The stairway came out on the street at the side of the building. Deadalus looked up and down the dark avenue, but their luck seemed to be holding. There was no sign of anybody. But when they got to the corner of the front of the building, Deadalus saw that there had been a third agent waiting at the bottom of the lift. That agent was now talking into a hand radio and Deadalus realized that he must be hearing from the agent up on Rhea's level who would have by this time realized that they had slipped through his fingers.

As Deadalus watched, he saw the agent motion to someone inside the building. Two local policemen came out and Deadalus could see the agent give them hurried instructions, pointing each one toward a corner of the building where they were evidently to stand guard.

Deadalus hurried Rhea back in the other direction. They went about fifty yards down the dark street and then he veered off on a small path that led down toward the water.

Docked along the edge of the canal were a number of private boats. Deadalus picked out the one which looked fastest and climbed aboard. Rhea followed wordlessly behind.

It took him a couple of minutes of cursing and mumbling threats before he figured out the controls to the boat, and even then Rhea had to show him which gauge indicated the fuel level.

As quietly as he could, Deadalus started the boat engine and backed out into the canal.

The dark waters of the canal lapped quietly at the side of the boat. For a moment Deadalus thought they were going to get away scot-free. Along the edge of the water, a few buildings had their lights on, but otherwise there was no sound of life except for the soft humming of their own engines.

But before he even had time to rev up the boat, a police cruiser came racing around the curve of the canal with a roar and brilliant floodlights.

Deadalus cursed. They would never be able to outrun the big boats. The only advantage he had was maneuverability. And he made the most of that.

Deadalus pushed the throttle to full and, spinning the nose of the boat around, headed directly for the big police cruiser. The police boat instinctively swerved to avoid the apparently imminent collision, and Deadalus shot past them. Deadalus glanced over his shoulder in time to see the big boat try to turn around. But because of its speed and the narrowness of the canal, its turn was too wide and, with a teeth-shuddering crash, it ran aground.

"Better get strapped in real tight," Deadalus called to Rhea, but then noticed that she was already belted down.

Far away now they could hear the rising sound of sirens as the alert went out. He was going to have to try and get as close to the spaceport as he could. They would most likely have to abandon the boat before too long. Their chances were better on foot, but the distance to the landing craft was still too far.

Deadalus had to keep his eyes on the canal as they raced at top speed through its narrow, winding unfamiliarity.

"Which way to the spaceport?" he called out over the roar of the engines.

"It's to the northeast, if that's any help."

Deadalus glanced quickly down at the ship's compass. They were heading north at the moment, but their direction changed radically every few hundred yards as the canal snaked and twisted around the odd-shaped islands. He was never going to be able to navigate like that.

Rhea reached over from the seat next to him and tapped him lightly on the shoulder.

"See those three red lights? That's the radio tower next to the ship field. Just aim for that."

Deadalus nodded but had no time to reply as a police cruiser came roaring out from a canal to their left and nearly ran them over.

Deadalus pretended that he was going to try and outrun the bigger ship, but as soon as he heard the cruiser throttle up, he slammed on the brakes and veered for the bank.

The cruiser roared right past them before the police pilot had time to react to Deadalus's maneuver. Deadalus started turning his small boat around, but the big boat had passed so close astern that its wake slammed Deadalus's boat into the docks.

Deadalus felt his teeth jar together from the blow. He was going to have to remember that this wasn't exactly the same thing as flying a spaceship. After the boat stopped rocking, Deadalus pushed the throttle to full, but he could feel that the crash had damaged something. The boat picked up sluggishly and the steering felt heavy.

As fast as he could, he headed back down a side canal, trying to get back in the right direction. But he could hear the siren of the police boat, which had turned around and was once again on their tail. He could also hear another siren approaching from the right.

Deadalus grinned.

There were some advantages to the boats. You sure would never hear a spaceship coming at you.

Deadalus slowed down enough for the boat behind to get them in its floodlight, then he pushed the boat to its top speed. The police pilot was being a bit more cautious now and, realizing that Deadalus didn't have that much speed, was taking care not to overrun them again.

There was a burst in the water to their left, but the shot came so close to the buildings on the shore that the police evidently thought better of it, and there were no more shots fired—much to Deadalus's relief.

He could now hear the siren on their left approaching. It had to be right around the next corner. Deadalus kept his course straight until the very last moment, then he dodged down the side canal, straight into the second cruiser, which was approaching at top speed. The cruiser spun as Deadalus's little boat flitted around it, but right at that moment the other cruiser came roaring around the corner.

The crash of the two police boats resulted in an enormous explosion. Deadalus could feel the heat from the fireball on the back of his neck, and small pieces of wreckage splashed in the water all around them.

Deadalus relocated the three red lights and

steered in their general direction. They were much closer now, but Deadalus could hear a number of sirens and could even make out the bright floodlights of some cruisers as they raced by on the other side of the island. They weren't going to make it all the way there, but Deadalus didn't necessarily want to anyway. There was no sense in showing the police exactly where they were going. They'd have to ditch the boat somewhere and take off on foot. It would take more time, but they would be harder to follow.

Deadalus looked around for some spot. The sirens and roar of engines were coming closer and seemed to be on every side.

"Hold on!" he yelled to Rhea and then slammed the boat into the shore.

A police cruiser caught up with them as they were extricating themselves from the wreckage. There were shots from some handguns as the cruiser came to a halt, but Deadalus didn't think that they were even trying to hit them, the shots went so wide.

While Rhea worked to unstrap herself, Deadalus aimed his laser at the police cruiser, trying for the fuel tanks. He was lucky and the tanks caught fire. They had to be some kind of solid fuel because they didn't explode as he had hoped, but instead burned with a blinding white glow as if they were magnesium.

As Deadalus helped Rhea up out of the boat, he saw that the policemen had run from their burning ship onto the shore opposite. But already he could hear more boats approaching. They turned and fled into the dark buildings of the island.

There seemed to be mostly industrial types of structures. They ran down the dark streets between the large, silent buildings. They started for a bridge that led to another island, but a band of policemen suddenly appeared on the other side. They ducked back down the way they had come, but they could now hear people approaching from that direction as well. Deadalus hurriedly led the way down another street only to find it a dead end. The sound of voices was quickly gaining on them.

Deadalus turned to the nearest doorway and blasted the lock off with his gun. They hurried inside and closed the door after them.

The building was completely black inside. For a minute Deadalus could not see anything at all. He stood with his back against the door, holding Rhea's hand so that she wouldn't get separated, and waited for his eyes to adjust.

Their heavy breathing sounded loud in the dark, strange building. Deadalus didn't at all like being inside. It was the easiest way to get trapped. But they hadn't had much of a choice. Things didn't seem to be going very well at all.

He mentally calculated how much time had elapsed. They were going to have to hurry if they wanted to make it to the spaceport before the two-hour limit he had given

Whiskey had expired. And even when they did get to the spaceport, it didn't mean they were home free. The two men who had chased them in Rhea's building had definitely been Secret Police. They were bound to have a ship at the port and they were now going to be on their guard.

Deadalus forced himself to forget his mounting feelings of frustration. He had to keep his head clear. When his eyes had adjusted a bit, he was able to make out a pale strip of light off in front of them. With his gun ready in one hand and the other tightly holding Rhea's, Deadalus started forward.

The floor underfoot was hard and dirty. He could feel sand or debris of some kind grating under his boot. There was also a strange acrid smell in the air. Some chemical that he couldn't name. Step by step he walked toward the light.

Suddenly the whole building was ablaze with light.

"Don't move or you're dead!" a voice to their right yelled out. That was the last mistake he ever made.

Deadalus shot instinctively and unerringly in the direction of the voice, at the same time pushing Rhea to the floor. He shot, dove, and shot again. But the second time proved to be unnecessary.

The man who turned out to be just a building guard was lying dead on the floor. Deadalus cursed the man's polite stupidity, but he had more to worry about than an amateur guard.

At the same time that the building lights had come on, an alarm had been triggered and there was the sound of running feet from the street outside the building.

Deadalus helped Rhea back to her feet and they ran toward a doorway on their left. Inside they found high rows of piled cartons evidently being stored. They ran down the aisles of stacks, looking for an exit. They heard the front door in the other room burst open. They ran deeper into the building. At the far side of the warehouse there were a number of doors, but none of them looked like they led outside. They ran along the wall, the sounds of voices getting ever closer.

In the middle of the wall was a sort of conveyor belt. Deadalus was helping Rhea to step over it when he realized that there was a cold, wet smell coming from the small tunnel that the belt led into. He looked in, but it was pitch black and he couldn't make out anything.

"Any idea where this might go?" he asked Rhea.

She looked at it skeptically and shook her head, not wasting her breath on words.

Deadalus shrugged and led the way in. There was a narrow walkway next to the track, only wide enough for one person to walk at a time. The roof was so low Deadalus almost had to stoop. The damp smell increased and, to his surprise, he found that the tunnel slanted down. He stopped, Rhea running into his back, and studied the situation.

He didn't like this at all. The downward slant of the tunnel gave him an uneasy feeling, almost claustrophobic. But the air wasn't stale, as he would expect if the tunnel was a dead end. It was moist and musty smelling, but it seemed to be moving, blowing lightly into his face.

He glanced back, and over Rhea's shoulder he could see that the lights were on in the warehouse they had just left. There was no turning back now. Quickly now he led the way forward.

The slant of the tunnel increased, as did its dampness. The floor now beneath their feet was wet and, when he touched the wall, he could feel beads of water.

Abruptly, the downward slant stopped and Deadalus could feel the air moving around him. In a few steps the tunnel began to slant upward at an even sharper incline than the downward had been. Ahead and above them Deadalus could distinctly make out the night sky and stars. He hurried.

Before they could even reach the end of the tunnel, the lights came on and the conveyor belt started up with a slow clanking. Deadalus pushed on as fast as he could, but the way was steep and the footing was wet and slippery. He glanced back and saw that Rhea was having an even harder time than he was, mostly because of the type of shoes she had on.

He got to the end of the tunnel and stumbled out, his gun ready. He found himself on a small island, no bigger than a platform. It was evidently some kind of loading area. The small island, which was probably manmade, had no other connection to the other land forms than the tunnel they had just come through. There were, however, a couple of flat barges docked along shore.

As he helped Rhea out, Deadalus could hear voices and footfalls from the other end of the tunnel. They ran over to the flatboats. One was full of water and, as he hurried Rhea into the other one, Deadalus realized that they weren't going to make it. These flatboats were too slow. The pursuers were too close behind. There was too much chance of getting caught out on the water by a police cruiser. Deadalus felt trapped and thought quickly through his options.

The thinking didn't take overlong, as the options were not that numerous.

"Rhea, listen. I'm going to have to slow down those guys in the tunnel. We'll never be able to get away otherwise."

"What are you going to do?"

"I'll see if I can't blow up a section of the tunnel and trap them in it. You keep low here in the barge. I'll be right back."

Rhea ducked low in the flatboat and watched Deadalus's dark outline as he ran back to the tunnel and disappeared down the opening as if into the mouth of some black beast.

Hunched down as low as she could go, Rhea concentrated on trying to get her breath back to normal while she waited. She kept herself from thinking. She just waited and watched.

Suddenly, without warning, there was a large explosion. It made Rhea start despite herself. The explosion had a strange, hollow, sucking sound and a moment later was followed by a billow of smoke, which came drifting almost lazily out of the mouth of the tunnel.

Rhea got ready to cast off at the first sign of Deadalus. She crouched, ready and waiting, her eyes searching in the smoke.

A minute passed.

The smoke passed and dissipated in the chill night air.

Another minute passed.

No one emerged from the tunnel.

Rhea hesitantly stood up, rocking the boat, hearing the small sound of the water lapping at its sides.

"Deadalus?" she called tremulously.

There was only silence.

chapter five

The agent came back into the cabin, wheeling a small, blue gray cart in front of him. The metal surface of the machine was covered with a number of gauges and knobs and buttons. From the side snaked three thick wires which ended in what was obviously a device meant to be placed on the victim's head.

Whiskey watched carefully as Dirk positioned the probe near his seat and turned it on. The agent adjusted a few of the knobs and then came over and put the headset on Whiskey.

The headset had a small hood which came down over his eyes so that he was unable to see. He could feel the top part being pressed down and there was the sharp pricking sensation of needles being pushed into his scalp.

Whiskey had no idea what a probe did. He had heard it mentioned once or twice in hushed tones but had never been able to develop a clear picture of exactly what it involved. He had no doubts as to its purpose though. It was simply an instrument of torture.

When the headset was in place, he heard Dirk move back over to the machine. Whiskey braced himself. Whatever they were going to do was going to be painful, that he was sure of. And another thing he was sure of was that when the questioning was over, he would be killed. The captain had called him by name. They knew he was from the *Orpheus*. They weren't going to let him live now that they knew.

Whiskey grit his teeth and prepared himself for whatever it was they had in store. As long as he kept in mind that he wasn't going to live no matter what he told them, as long as he remembered that there was nothing he could say that could buy his way back to life, he was pretty sure that he would be able to withstand their torture without giving them the information they wanted. He'd been subjected to pain before. He knew that he could withstand a great deal of it. He also knew that what really made torture unbearable was not so much the pain, but the thought that your torturers would kill you unless you answered their questions, and that once you did, they might let you live.

So Whiskey tried to keep his mind firm on

the thought that no matter what he did they were going to kill him anyway. There was no way that they would leave him alive. In their minds he had committed the foulest crime possible—he'd been a party to the killing of members of their corps. It was unheard of to kill a member of the Secret Police. And it was even more unheard of to live after you'd done so.

The captain's voice broke into his thoughts. "You're going to tell us what we want to know, Whiskey. Sooner or later. There's no way out of it. Why don't you save yourself this ordeal? You'll gain nothing by it. No one is going to know how much pain you were able to bear before breaking. No one's going to applaud the fact that you allowed yourself to be subjected to the most horrendous agony possible, just so that you could hold onto your information for two or three minutes longer. You don't owe this to anyone. Why don't you just answer our questions?"

Whiskey said nothing. It seemed like a strange sort of courteous ritual that the captain was performing, like granting one last request to a man before you shot him. It really didn't make any sense. Whiskey knew that the captain had no intention of sparing him any pain. Why pretend to? It seemed to Whiskey that they would be better off by trying to scare him, not console him.

Whiskey heard a hum as the machine was adjusted. He wondered what it could possibly do to him. He'd heard all sorts of frightening stories when he was younger about the terrible form of torture that the Empirical Secret Police practiced. He'd even seen a picture once of a man who'd had a whole layer of skin stripped from his face. The man had lived for over a month like that, he'd been told. He never did find out how the police had managed such a feat. Perhaps that was what this probe did. Maybe it electrically blistered your skin so that it separated and peeled off. Probably not. That sounded too simple, too neat, and not painful enough.

The humming sound raised in frequency.

"Deadalus doesn't care about you," the captain's voice said, surprisingly near Whiskey's ear. "Where is he now? He let you walk into this. He's not here to help you. What do you owe him? Holding back any information isn't going to help him now. Where is he?"

Whiskey would have spat in reply, if his mouth weren't so dry. Why didn't they get on with it? Why were they just fooling around? Did the stupid machine really take that long to get warmed up? Why didn't they let Bull kick and punch him around for a while until it was ready then? This waiting was getting to be a real pain. His stomach was in a hard knot, ready at any moment for a jolt from the machine. It would be easier if he had some idea of the kind of torture they were going to use. It would be easier to prepare for it.

Whiskey recalled some of the other stories

he'd heard about their torture. One man, it was said, had had his hand stuck in a cage with a hungry rat and had to sit there and watch as the rat ate his hand down to the bare bone. It was said that the man had lived through the whole ordeal, but that he'd finally gone crazy from the sound of the rat continually gnawing on the bones.

Or there was the other story about the man who'd had a small hole burned in his lower stomach, from which the agents pulled his entire intestinal tract, inch by inch. And when that was completely exposed, they started on the other organs, carefully keeping the man alive.

Whiskey wondered how this Captain Webern had found out who he was. The agents had seemed to be going for his story until he'd come in with his questions about the gun and such. How had he known? Had he been tipped off? Or maybe Deadalus had been already apprehended. The agents had mentioned that someone was going after the girl, maybe they already had Deadalus. Maybe Deadalus had already been forced to talk. That would be some joke. Here he was holding out his information, going through their various tortures, and maybe Deadalus had already talked.

Whiskey cursed himself angrily. That was stupid. If Deadalus had already talked, why would they be questioning him at all? If they'd already apprehended Deadalus, they'd just be turning him over a slow fire, taking pleasure no doubt in causing him pain, but not wasting their time by questioning him. As long as they kept asking him questions, he could be sure that Deadalus was still beyond their reach.

But why didn't they get on with it? What was taking them so long? Whiskey would have shouted at them to hurry up if he hadn't already decided to remain absolutely silent under all circumstances. He wasn't scared of their pain. He could take pain. But why didn't they hurry up and get it over with? They knew they were going to kill him. He knew that they were going to kill him. Why were they persisting in this nonsense?

The pitch of the humming increased as if just to make sure he knew that it was still there.

"Why don't you just tell us what we want to know, Whiskey?" It was the captain's voice again. "You don't owe anybody the type of torture we have in mind for you. You've paid your dues. You've done all you could. Now why don't you just tell us where Deadalus is? That's all we want to know. Just tell us and we won't have to go through with this. You can tell us now or you can tell us in a few minutes. What's the difference? You won't be doing anyone any good by going through what's coming. So why not just tell us now where Deadalus is?"

Whiskey set his jaw, trying to drive out the sound of the captain's voice. It was making too much sense. Why should he let them put his hand in a rat cage or something? If they'd sent men out to take Pablo's daughter, they'd know soon enough where Deadalus was anyway. If that's all they wanted, why shouldn't he tell them?

Behind the humming sound he heard another noise. He imagined a small cage being readied. He imagined a rat, kept unfed for a week, scratching and clawing in hunger at its cage. Whiskey sniffed, he could almost smell the heavy scent of a rodent.

A sweat broke out on his face. They probably had something even worse intended. Something which he couldn't even imagine. Something which no one had ever lived to talk about. They would either extract the information they wanted out of him by torture, or he would die in the process. Either way they'd kill him when this was over. Giving them the information would not save his life. But if he told them all he knew, maybe they'd hurry up. Maybe they'd kill him quick and simply. Maybe they wouldn't need to use this probe, whatever it was. Or the rat's cage. Or whatever horrendous thing they had in store. All they wanted to know was where Deadalus was. It was almost funny. He could tell them that without even really compromising anything. When it came right down to it, he didn't really know anything that would be of much use to them. He knew that Deadalus had gone after the girl and was to meet him at the spaceport. But they'd have that figured out pretty soon anyway, after they heard from the men that they'd sent after the doctor's daughter. They'd know that Deadalus had her. They'd know that the only place he could go with her is back here to the spaceport. Maybe they already knew that.

Whiskey's mind was filled with the images of a rat's yellow eyes, its long teeth. He could clearly picture it as if it was being displayed on a screen in front of him. He could imagine his hand being inserted into the cage. He could almost feel the teeth riping hungrily into his flesh, peeling the skin down off his fingers, lapping at the spurting red blood. He could clearly imagine how, after eating half his hand, the rat would sit back, momentarily full and contented. Whiskey could picture the bones of his fingers sticking bare and white out of the ruined flesh. He could imagine how cold the air would be on the clean tips of his finger bones.

The picture was so distinct in his mind that Whiskey didn't even notice that the humming of the machine again increased in pitch, raising to a level just within hearing range.

Whiskey's teeth were chattering. He fought to control himself, to push the image of the rat out of his mind. But as soon as it did, more images filled its place. Strange horrendous things dredged up from out of all his worst nightmares. And all the while a voice in the back of his head kept repeating that all he had to do was tell them what they wanted to know. Tell them, and then he'd be set free into the painlessness of death.

He wasn't going to gain anything by holding out. No one would even know. And even if they did know how long he lasted, would they praise him for having withstood five or six minutes of agony? Everyone knew that he was brave. But even the bravest, most determined men would break.

A sense of urgency filled him along with the nightmares in his mind. He had to stop them before they got started. Then it would be irreversible. If he told them the little that they wanted to know, then they'd kill him. And death, in the face of all the tortures he was imagining, would be a blessing.

"Where is Deadalus?"

The question came through the horrendous images that filled his mind almost as if it were a part of them.

"He went to get the girl," Whiskey thought. Or did he say it out loud? He couldn't tell. His mind was too filled with images of rats and men with skinless faces and intestines being slowly twisted out of his body.

"What's Deadalus doing on Meer?"

"Trying to save the doctor's daughter," Whiskey mumbled. The images in his mind had become so real it almost seemed to him that a large rat was questioning him. He had the feeling that if he told the rat everything it wanted to know, it would kill him. And right now he was wishing he were dead.

"Why is he saving the doctor's daughter?"

"The doctor asked him to."

"Why?"

"He wouldn't leave without her." Whiskey mumbled as quickly as he could. Time seemed to be running out.

"What does Deadalus want with the doctor?" It was the captain's voice, but it sounded a little shrill.

"He doesn't want the doctor to get hurt," Whiskey replied as honestly as he could.

"Why?"

"Because he's an old friend." The questions didn't seem to make any sense, but Whiskey answered as best he could. If that's all they wanted to know, he'd be more than happy to answer.

"Where's the *Orpheus*?"

"I don't know."

Suddenly the nightmares in his head increased in intensity.

"Where's the *Orpheus*?" the question was repeated.

Whiskey thought, but he didn't know where the *Orpheus* was.

"I don't know. It's no place. It's just moving around."

"Where is it moving around?"

Whiskey could hardly make any sense of the question. He thought as hard as he could, trying to come up with the right answer.

"In space?" he asked hopefully.

He felt a new wave of depression wash over him. This whole thing was stupid. It was just a childish game that had gotten out of hand. What had Deadalus intended to do with the starship anyway? Who did he hope to fight and conquer? It was all just a stupid game and Whiskey wanted to stop playing.

"How were you to get back to the starship?"

"In the *Ezra*."

"What's the *Ezra?*"

"One of the *Orpheus*'s landing craft."

"Where is it now?"

"Here at the spaceport."

"Which dock number?"

Whiskey thought hard, trying to remember the number. He wanted to tell them what they wanted to know, he wanted to satisfy them so that they wouldn't use the probe on him. That's all that mattered now.

"Number one-four-two. I think."

"And how were you to contact the *Orpheus?*"

"The captain was going to call it. On the radio."

"How?"

"I . . . I don't know. Deadalus was to do that. He didn't tell me. Honestly."

"Where was the *Orpheus* headed after here?"

"I don't know. Nowhere. He didn't say."

Desperately Whiskey tried to think of the right answer. The questions seemed so meaningless. And it seemed even more meaningless that he had been about to let them torture him in order not to tell them.

Now all he was worrying about was answering as quickly as possible. The image of the rat gnawing on his hand was still strong in his mind. It seemed as if he could hear them bringing the cage, could hear the scamper of the rat's sharp claws against the metal, could even smell the strong odor of the beast.

"Where is the *Orpheus* headed? What are it's plans?"

"Nowhere. Nothing. There are no plans." Whiskey was almost yelling in his desperation to make himself believed. He was horrified that they might think he was still trying to hide some information. He was actually shaking in agitation. They were still going to torture him. Even now. Even after all this. They didn't believe his answer. They were going to turn the probe on. They were going to put his hand in the rat's cage. They were going to do even more, unimaginable things.

"Believe me! Believe me!" he yelled, then fainted from sheer terror.

chapter six

The smell of the smoke was still sharp in the cold night air. Rhea stood in the boat which rocked gently in the water. Far away she could hear the siren of a police cruiser rise and fall like the wail of a motherless child.

"Deadalus?" she called, her voice hardly louder than the soft slap of the water against the boat.

There was no answer, no movement from the small tunnel.

Rhea stepped out of the boat and back onto the small piece of land. She tightly crossed her arms, trying to calm the trembling that had come over her. Carefully, quietly, she stepped toward the tunnel where Deadalus had disappeared.

She got to its mouth and looked in. The lights had gone back out and the conveyor belt had stopped. The smell of the explosion was even stronger. She listened. All she could hear was the sound of dripping water from somewhere down in the tunnel.

She started down the tunnel, then stopped.

Perhaps that was the wrong thing to do. Deadalus had told her to wait. Perhaps he was lying low, trying to draw their fire, trying to make sure that none of them had survived. Perhaps if she went in the tunnel now, she would jeopardize him. Maybe even get him killed. He had instructed her to wait in the boat. She should do as he said.

But what if he was lying in there hurt? What if he needed her help desperately? He had been in such a hurry. What if something had gone wrong, something unexpected. He might even be dead. He wouldn't wait in there, silent and unanswering, unless something was wrong. They had to get away. They had to hurry. He would have come right back out. If he was able to.

Tremulously she started down the damp walkway. It was pitch black. She couldn't even make out where to put her feet and had to walk slowly so as not to trip on any of the rubble that now littered the wet floor.

Her breath came in short gasps. She was afraid to call out again. What if Deadalus had gotten killed and there were just policemen silently waiting until they knew exactly where she was so that they could shoot her. Or worse. What if they wanted to finish what they had started back at her apartment.

She stopped. Maybe she should just get away as fast as she could. If Deadalus was dead, she'd have to fend for herself. And the sooner she got away from here the better.

She could go to the spaceport and find her father.

She shook her head, angry at herself. How could she even think of leaving before she found out for certain what had happened to Deadalus. If he was dead, she'd have to make certain before she did anything else. And perhaps he wasn't dead at all, but only hurt or trapped. How could she even consider running away.

Rhea continued down the slippery path much quicker now. After all, Deadalus had saved her life. If she got killed trying to help him, it would be an even return.

There was more rubble the farther that she ventured down the tunnel. In the darkness it became very difficult to move very fast. At first she tried to make as little noise as possible, but this soon became impossible. She clambered over the fallen beams and construction material that littered the floor and conveyor track.

It seemed like she had gone much farther than Deadalus could possibly have gone before the explosion. Even given his quicker speed, he wouldn't have gone any farther than the low point in the tunnel. And she must be nearly there by now. Perhaps she had somehow passed him already.

She decided that she would continue down to the low point and, if she hadn't come across him by then, she would turn around and search back a little ways.

But shortly, Rhea came to a mound of

fallen material that seemed to completely block the small tunnel. She felt over its surface with her hands but could find no way through it at all. She leaned against its wet surface and thought.

Deadalus's plan of blocking the tunnel had worked. Hopefully, he had caught most of the policemen inside. Otherwise they would have called a patrol boat by now to get to the island from the surface. If they had, she was as good as caught.

But where was Deadalus? Did he get caught on the other side of the blockage? Or underneath it?

The sound of dripping water brought her out of her thoughts, and she peered up at the ceiling of the tunnel, trying to see what kind of condition it was in. She had suddenly realized that it must be underwater at this point. If the roof had been too greatly weakened by the explosion, it could come crashing in at any moment, letting loose a flood of water. Rhea shivered.

"Deadalus!" she said loudly, realizing that there was nothing to be gained by remaining silent. There obviously were no policemen on this side of the rubble or they would have shot her or something by now.

"Deadalus!" she called again even louder.

She held her breath and listened.

There was the continual sound of dripping water. Then, somewhere in the impenetrable blackness of the tunnel, there was another sound. It sounded like a cough, or a groan maybe.

"Deadalus? Deadalus, where are you?"

This time the groan was plainly audible. As well as a few choice curses.

Rhea felt her heart leap as she recognized Deadalus's voice somewhere close by.

"Deadalus, say something so I can find you. It's me, Rhea." She realized how silly this last sounded, but she was in no position to worry about it now.

"I'm right over here," Deadalus said. His voice sounded alright, if a little disgusted.

Rhea made her way back through the rubble toward him. She finally located him in the blackness. He was lying wedged in on the other side of the conveyor track, completely covered with rubble.

"Deadalus! Are you alright? Are you hurt?"

"I'm afraid my leg has suffered some. Can't tell how much, as it's still numb from shock. But otherwise I seem to be alive."

Rhea started clearing the heavy rubble off of him as quickly and carefully as she could. She got his chest and arms cleared enough so that he could help her.

"This damn tunnel sure isn't built very well. Don't you guys know how to make cement on Meer? The explosive I set off shouldn't have been enough to do any structural damage at all. I had caught them all bunched together and tried to just kill enough of them to put a damper on their pursuit.

But then the whole damn tunnel caved in on top of us."

As he talked in an obviously disgusted tone, he helped clear off all the rubble but the one large piece which was on top of his leg, pinning it against the track. His angle on it was poor, he couldn't give Rhea much help.

The girl pulled at it and pushed at it and kicked it, but it didn't budge. It was just too heavy.

"If I had some kind of pulley system," she muttered, looking around. "Have you a belt or something, Deadalus?"

"No. Besides, there's nothing to hook it to. The ceiling is all cement. Albeit, poor-quality cement."

Deadalus had a sick feeling in the pit of his stomach. The feeling was beginning to come back into his leg now, and the feeling wasn't good. The leg felt pretty smashed. Even if they did manage to get the piece of rubble off, he wasn't going to be able to move very fast. If at all.

"I think you ought to go and get Whiskey," he said.

"Fine time to think of drinking," she muttered.

"No. Whiskey, he's my second in command. He's with your father at the spaceport."

"I'm not going without you."

"Listen, Rhea, I don't think we can get that stupid stone off my leg. And if we can, I won't be able to move fast enough."

"Of course we can get it off," she replied, moving away in the darkness. "All I need is some kind of lever or something."

Rhea searched through the rubble for something to use as a lever. She felt along the conveyor tracks, but there was nothing suitable there. Even if there had been, it would have probably taken as long to loosen it as get the stone off. She felt along the black floor with her hands, trying desperately to find something, anything.

The floor was covered with two inches of water. She searched over and under the rubble but could find nothing.

"Maybe I could use the boat," she suggested. "I could attach a long rope to the stone and haul it off with the boat."

"We don't have a long rope, Rhea."

"Well, there's got to be some way!" she snapped, her voice showing both fear and anger over Deadalus's lack of suggestions.

She came back and tried once again to force the piece of rubble off of Deadalus's leg.

Deadalus calculated in his mind what the time must be. He realized that even if he hadn't been unconscious for very long, and he had no way of knowing how long he'd been out, there was very little time left before Whiskey blasted off.

"How long was it after the explosion before you found me?" he asked.

"I don't know. Ten minutes maybe."

"Well there's still a little time then. I want

you to go to the spaceport and get Whiskey. I gave him instructions when I left him with your father that he was to blast off in two hours whether we were there or not. The time's almost up. It'll be no use getting me free if we don't get to the spaceport in time. And even if you could get that thing off my leg, I wouldn't be able to move fast enough."

Rhea, who had stopped for the moment to rest, was breathing heavily as she listened to him.

"I'm not going anywhere without you," she said, her voice low and determined.

"Damnit! You've got to. If Whiskey blasts off, it will be hours before I can get him back down. And I doubt if he is going to able to evade the Secret Police for that long. You've got to go and stop him. He'll come back with you and help you get me loose."

"I don't want to just leave you here like this," she argued plantively.

"The only way you're going to do me any good at all is to do exactly what I say," he said sternly. "Here, take this gun and get to the spaceport as quickly as you can. The ship is called the *Ezra* and it's in dock one-four-two. Tell Whiskey exactly what's happened. He'll decide how and what to do from there. And if he decides that you should stay at the ship while he comes back, or even if he for some reason decides to blast off without coming back for me, I want you to do what he says. You understand? The only way we can hope to do any good is with a team effort, and to do that you need to know how to follow orders. Is that clear?"

"Yes, sir." Rhea's voice was slightly mocking and somewhat chagrined. She took the gun he handed her.

"That's a good kid."

Dcadalus waited for the sound of her departure and was surprised when he felt her lean over and kiss him on the forehead. Then he heard the sound of her sloshing back up the tunnel.

He lay back with a slight groan. The pain in his leg had increased. He felt around as best he could, but he wasn't able to determine what the extent of the damage was. He pushed halfheartedly on the stone, but it didn't budge.

Sighing, he tried to get into as comfortable position as possible. The water, which was now about six inches deep, was cold and made him all the more uncomfortable.

Farther down in the tunnel there was the continual sound of dripping water.

Glancing up toward the exit, Deadalus was discouraged to find that he was able to make out the small patch of lightening sky. Dawn was not far off.

chapter seven

Rhea climbed into the flatboat and pushed off. She worked the controls until she got the engine started, then she turned the heavy barge toward the spaceport and throttled the sluggish engines as high as they could go.

Her teeth were chattering and she wasn't sure if it was from cold or from the emotional strain. Probably both. She looked around in the boat for something to try and keep the cold wind off with. She found a thick, heavy bargman's jacket behind one of the seats. She put the damp-smelling thing on and turned up the collar. That at least solved the problem of the cold.

She fiddled with the controls but was unable to get the boat to go any faster than a slow crawl. The barge was designed for hauling heavy loads and just could not go fast. Keeping her eyes on the water, Rhea tried to sort out some of the things that had happened in the last few hours.

The news about how deep in trouble her father was worried her. He never confided in her anything that might cause her to get upset, and therefore she had had no real idea as to the extent of his problem. But Deadalus had made it quite clear that her father would probably be killed if ever captured by the Secret Police.

Despite her worries, Rhea knew that her father could take care of himself. He had told her many times about the nature of the people he was working with. He had brought her up knowing that to deal with the Secret Police always involved great risks. Deadalus hadn't been specific as to the nature of the information which her father was trying to hide, but he obviously knew what the results would be. He took the chances at his own risk and he could take care of himself.

Right at the moment Rhea was more concerned about Deadalus. Trapped the way he was, he was at the mercy of any policemen who happened by. She had to get some help and get him out of there. He had saved her from those policemen. It was for her sake that he was now caught under that rock, his leg smashed and him practically unable to defend himself.

The thought about what had happened at her apartment earlier made her feel nauseated. She pressed her hand to her head and forced the image of the blood and gore out of her mind. It was too much for her to deal with. Maybe at some other time when she was safe and there was nothing else to worry about she could try and come to terms with what had happened. But she couldn't think about it now. She couldn't think about anything except what she had to do to get help for Deadalus.

She had not really been surprised when Deadalus had shown up at her apartment to save her. That was just the kind of thing she always expected of him. All her life he had been a cross between a white knight and an endearing uncle to her. She had heard the rumors just like everyone else about how he had defected from the Secret Police. And then the stories which followed each other as regularly as the sunsets about how he was killed here, taken prisoner and tortured to death there, lost amid an asteroid shower somewhere else. She had listened carefully to each story and then dismissed it, more amused than really worried. She was not the least bit surprised to find out that he was indeed still alive. And that he would show up here to help her and her father in their desperate trouble was just his nature. She wouldn't expect any less from him.

But she realized that it was more than old friendship that she felt at the moment. She'd had a crush on Deadalus for as long as she had known him. And instead of dissipating as she got older, the crush had matured right along with her womanhood. He was an ideal to her. She had spent her life trying to live up to that ideal. Trying to stay fit, trying to keep her mind as sharp as his, trying to keep that same style of dry humor in even the most dire situations. And now was her chance to act.

And as of yet, she thought wryly, she'd been nothing but trouble.

She heard the loud roar of a boat approaching her from the rear and, glancing back, she saw the lights of a police patrol boat.

She looked around desperately trying to think of what she should do. The flat barge was no competition, even if she had Deadalus's skill in maneuvering. There was no way to run and no place to hide.

So she decided to do just the opposite.

As the police boat approached, she choked the engines, making them come to a sputtering stop. Then, making sure that the collar on the big jacket was turned up, disguising her face and form, she turned on the boat's lights and bent over as if examining the engines. The police boat pulled up alongside and slowed down, turning its floodlight on her.

Excitedly, Rhea waved the boat over, as if asking for a hand. She pointed to the engines, indicating that she was having a problem, and then called out gruffly over the roar of the other boat's engines.

"Hey, how 'bout a hand here? Got some

problem. Only take you a few minutes. How about it?"

The floodlight snapped off and the police boat sped off as if disgusted at its wasted time.

Rhea shook her fist after them like an angry barge operator and laughed. The ruse had worked. Had she tried to run, they would have chased her. But it was too inconceivable to them that anyone scared of the police would flag them over and ask for help.

Rhea was momentarily pleased with her quick thinking. But then she angrily started the engines back up and scolded herself. There was still a lot more to be done before she was safe. She shouldn't waste time praising herself over one little battle.

It seemed like nearly forever before she reached the spaceport. The sky was noticeably beginning to lighten as she circled the island heading for the front entrance. She had no idea whether or not she would be able to just walk right in, but it was by far the simplest thing, and so she thought she might as well check it out first.

As she rounded the corner of the island, she saw that the front gate was crowded with police vehicles and that there were numerous uniformed men running about here and there. Evidently the straightforward manner wasn't going to work here.

She turned the heavy barge around and slowly circled the island, looking for some kind of opening. There was no kind of barrier visible from the water, but she knew that there was an electronic fence up on the bank. And possibly there was even other surveillance equipment that she didn't know about.

She thought about it a little and then dismissed it as something she just couldn't worry about. She wasn't going to be able to use the front gate. If she was going to get to the ship and talk to Whiskey, she was going to have to try and get in over the fence. There really didn't seem to be any other choice.

She found a low indentation in the island and docked the boat. She took off the heavy jacket and climbed up the steep bank to the perimeter walkway to look around. She could see no one on the path and so she stepped out onto it. On the other side of the path was the fence, which consisted of a series of steel poles with apparent emptiness between them. This was a simple electromagnetic-field barrier. Familiar with such things, Rhea knew that they were about a foot thick and provided a strong electrical shock if breached. The voltage of the shock was dependent on the size of body that went into the field and the distance in it went. Thus the fence was able to keep out animals and people without killing them. If one accidently walked into the fence, he would only get a mild shock, just strong enough to discourage further penetration. But if one tried to force his way through, the electrical shock would be enough to kill.

Rhea checked out the equipment and then stood back to think. There had to be some way to get through the field without getting killed. She had had the best training possible in field theory from her father. Surely some of that knowledge should turn up something useful.

She paced back and forth, keeping her eyes open for any sign of police or guards, and thinking. Then she got an idea.

She took out the gun Deadalus had forced upon her and, after checking to make sure she was using it right, fired at a spot just inside the fence. The laser went through without any problem. There were a few sparks where it contacted the field, but nothing else.

Rhea walked quickly alongside the fence until she found what she was looking for. About every hundred yards the fence was connected to a simple induction coil. There was no other way to maintain a high enough charge over the whole length of the fence. The coil was in a small black box about thirty feet inside the fence. Rhea figured that she should be able to burn it out with the laser. With the coil out, the shock of the field might be small enough to withstand.

There was of course the possibility that there was some kind of warning system that would go off any time the fence had been tampered with. But Rhea just didn't see what other choice she had. And time was getting very short.

She held the gun with both hands and fired. It wasn't a particularly difficult shot and she had no problem hitting the black box. She held the laser steady until it had burned through the box. There was a sudden hissing and popping and a number of sparks shot out. Rhea looked at the fence but was unable to see anything different. She gingerly stuck her hand into the field closest to the box.

There was a slight tingling, but not at all the customary jolt. Carefully she stepped forward. The tingling increased. She hesitated.

The force field was at least a foot thick and she was only inches into it. What would happen when she got all the way in? Would there still be enough force left in it to kill her?

She stepped back out of the fence and quickly bent over, searching in the plants next to the pathway. In a moment she stood up, triumphantly holding one of the large beetles which plagued Meer's vegetation.

She walked back over to the fence and gently tossed the bug through the field. It twisted about for a moment when it landed as if in pain, but then it resolutely got up and scurried away, physically undamaged. Rhea happily started to walk through after it, but halfway through, the electrical sensation was too much for her. She backed out, got a running start, and leaped through.

She rolled as she landed and came quickly to her feet, looking around to see if there was anybody there to notice her. She felt alright: a funny sensation in her stomach was the only ill effect of the fence.

Rhea looked around, memorizing the nearby area so that she would be able to get back out the same way she'd come in, if necessary, and then hurried toward the ships she could see a few hundred yards ahead.

After a brief strip of ground around the perimeter, the entire island was paved and marked off in various sections. The area was at the moment well lit, a bright white glow in the dark sky. There seemed to be a lot of activity on the ground but, Rhea noticed, there didn't seem to be any ships taking off or landing. Nor had there been for quite a while.

It wasn't really that surprising. After what had happened at her apartment, there was probably a general alert out for her and Deadalus and they were no doubt keeping all the ships grounded just to make sure that they didn't get away. It could greatly complicate matters though in regard to Deadalus's man in charge of the ship. He may have become aware of the impending grounding and blasted off, trying to at least get her father out of reach of the Secret Police.

If that was the case, she would just have to go back and help Deadalus by herself. She was sure she could find something to take with her that would aid in getting the stone off his leg. And then ... well, they'd just have to see.

There seemed to be a great number of uniformed men milling about among the ships. But there were quite a number of other people as well. The confusion looked as if it would be sufficent enough to cover her as she made her way to the landing craft.

Checking off the numbers as she went, she stayed as out of sight as she could. She could not see any pattern or purpose to all the people wandering around. The grounding had evidently caused problems for those with legitimate reasons for wanting to take off. These people were just walking around grumbling and glaring as if they would be able to browbeat the authorities into rescinding their orders. All the uniformed policemen who were briskly walking here and there were probably doing nothing more than making their presence felt as a sort of deterrent.

Rhea got to the row on which the *Ezra* was parked. It was still there, she could see it sitting quietly in its dock. The only trouble was that there was a police barrier around it and half a dozen policemen standing guard.

It was impossible to see if anyone was on board from this distance, so Rhea snuck around to try and get a closer look.

Standing next to a nearby ship, Rhea saw the *Ezra*'s port door open and three men descend the ramp. Two of the men were local police. The third was the agent that had chased them through the apartment complex.

Rhea bit her lip anxiously. Where were her father and Deadalus's man, Whiskey? Had they managed to hide someplace? Or were they already prisoners of the Secret Police?

There was no time for her to worry about it now. She couldn't go looking for them. She was going to see about helping Deadalus by herself.

She had just turned to leave when a huge, heavy hand clamped down on her shoulder. She started and looked over her shoulder to find herself looking into the fat face of an overweight police officer. The officer was smiling.

"My, my," he said, smacking his lips. "What have we here?"

chapter eight

Whiskey had the feeling of a man who is waiting to throw up. He knew that it was coming. He knew it was unavoidable. And, though he wasn't looking forward to it, he knew that he would feel better once it had been done.

All of a sudden he was hauled out of the seat and propped precariously on his feet. He wobbled from side to side and would have fallen had not Bull taken hold of his shoulder. Whiskey knew what was coming. They were going to kill him. He had served his puny purpose and now they were just going to get rid of him.

His head felt very groggy and his breathing was coming hard, as if he'd just gone through a strenuous exercise. All his muscles ached from tension. In a way it would be a relief to be killed.

Nothing made much sense at the moment. He could comprehend what was happening; he just couldn't see the purpose behind any of it. Bull was holding him up by the shoulder. The captain was looking at him somewhat annoyed and perhaps a little surprised. He was saying something about taking him to the *Ezra*. But he couldn't really figure it out. And Whiskey didn't really care.

All he knew was that he had told them all they had asked for, he had answered every one of their questions, and he had done so from his own free will. They had not even needed to torture him. Like a little kid, he had become so scared of the vague fantasies of what the probe might do, he had told them all he knew before they even had to use it.

Now they were leading him out of the spaceship. It was still night, but the spaceport lights were dimming against a brightening sky. There were hundreds of people milling around, all of them looking like they had nothing to do but stare at him. He supposed that it was only natural. A dead man often draws attention. And he was certain that he was as good as dead. That's all that was left for him. That was all he really wanted. He didn't want to play in this game anymore. He didn't want to fight and kill and run and hide. It was too much for him. He couldn't take it anymore.

He was led down the ship ramp, Bull holding him up on one side and Dirk on the other. His own hands were still bound behind his back, but that was alright. He had no use for them anyway. He hardly even felt like lifting up and putting down his feet, step after step.

The cold air helped to clear his head and he became more aware of what was going on. The two agents were taking him to the *Ezra*. He tried to remember why. Slowly, as if dredging the memory up out of an old nightmare, Whiskey recalled that the captain had said something about taking the *Ezra* with them, and that Whiskey should be kept aboard it.

The Secret Police knew about the landing craft because he himself had told them, of course. Whiskey tried to recall his thoughts that had led up to his being willing to answer the captain's questions. But the thoughts had been too jumbled. All he could get was a strange picture of a wild type of nightmare, and even that was enough to make his mind shy away from pursuing the thought.

He had broken. That's all there was to it. They had broken him with just the threat of torture. It almost seemed impossible, but that's what had happened.

A residue of fear shuddered through him

and, had the agent not been holding him up, Whiskey would have buckled. He didn't want to walk, he didn't want to move. He just wanted to lie down and let the world go on without him.

As Dirk and Bull approached the *Ezra*, holding the limp Whiskey up between them, they were stopped by a man who wore the uniform of a port authority.

"Are you the two representatives from the Empirical Police?" the man asked somewhat pompously.

Bull grunted.

"Yeah," Dirk replied, a little more coherently than his partner. "What's the problem?"

"I've just been told that you've intentions of taking this ship here," he pointed over his shoulder to where the *Ezra* was standing.

"Yeah. So?"

"Well I'm afraid that's impossible."

"Impossible? What are you talking about? That ship belongs to us. It's an Empirical Police vehicle. Why shouldn't we take it."

The man hemmed and hawed for a moment, looking very uneasy.

"It may be as you say, but it came here registered under the name of Pepper."

"It was stolen. We're simply taking it back."

"I'm afraid that's not the way we do things here on Meer. That may be your practice back on Earth, I really don't know. But here we provide a proper system of justice.

If that's your ship, you'll have to go through the local authorities in order to state your claim."

Bull grunted again, this time more threateningly.

"Why? I don't see where it's any of your business if we wish to repossess one of our own ships."

"Oh, but it is. You see, I'm the port authority here and . . ."

"Yes, I can see that," Dirk said sarcastically.

"Yes. Well, it seems this ship still owes it's docking dues. It's our right to impound any vehicle until the proper dues are met. In case they aren't, under section five-two-eight, subsection seven, we are given the right to sell any such vehicle for the amount of port dues owed."

Dirk let go of Whiskey and stepped closer to the port authority. He was a good six inches taller than the other man, and the look on the agent's face was not pleasant.

"You can take your stinking little codes and . . ."

"I'll have you know they're the Empirical codes!" the man suddenly snapped back. "And you are Empirical citizens the same as the rest of us. You are not going to come barging in here with your high-handed ways and think that you can just do what you please. You're supposed to be upholding the laws, not breaking them."

The little man seemed genuinely irate. Dirk

stared at him for a minute, then shook his head with a low curse.

"Maybe you'd better talk to the captain," he said.

"Yes, maybe I'd just better do that."

"I'll be right back," Dirk called over his shoulder as he led the insistent little man back toward the Secret Police ship.

Just then a policeman walked up to Bull and Whiskey.

"Hey, I think I've got that girl you were looking for," he said with a grin.

Her arms in the tight grip of the policeman's fat hands, Rhea glared at the two men in front of her.

Deadalus shook his head in disgust. This was one of the stupidest positions he had ever found himself in. Bad enough to be stuck under the piece of rubble like a bug under a rock, but now the water had risen up to his chest and showed every sign of continuing until it had filled the entire tunnel.

He shifted his position, trying to keep his head as high as possible. The cold water did have a beneficial side effect though. It had so chilled him that his leg was only a throbbing ache rather than the sharp pain it had been earlier.

Deadalus didn't worry himself by trying to think of all the things that could so easily get in the way of his being rescued. Rhea would either get back with Whiskey in time or she wouldn't. There wasn't anything he could do about it either way.

Deadalus looked up toward the tunnel entrance, where he could see the sky turning light blue with the dawn.

Down below him the dripping sound of water continued.

chapter nine

They all stood motionless for a moment, as if waiting for time and fate to catch up with them.

Rhea glaring at the hideous-looking man in front of her who was nearly carrying the other man.

The big policeman was beaming with self-importance at having captured the girl that the Secret Police were looking for.

Whiskey, completely limp, his bemused expression momentarily replaced by a sharp look of interest.

Bull, holding up the limp prisoner, confused by all the things that had happened at the same time, staring at the good-looking girl in the policeman's grasp.

They stood like that for the space of a breath.

Then Bull broke the spell. He turned back to yell after Dirk and the port authority. He yelled once, but Dirk was evidently too far away to hear him and didn't turn around. As he stared over his shoulder, behind him a number of things happened at the same time.

The overweight policeman, feeling as if he was being offhandedly dismissed by Bull, let go of Rhea and stood back, angry at having his big success go so unnoticed.

Rhea, who had been waiting for some opening, reached for the gun that was still hidden in her clothes. The fat policeman had not searched her, either because she was just a girl or from plain lack of intelligence.

Whiskey was watching her sharply and he didn't miss the unmistakable motion as she reached for a gun. The policeman had identified her for him, and Whiskey's head had suddenly become clear. If the girl was here, that meant that Deadalus was somewhere close by. As Rhea pulled out the gun, Whiskey sprang to life. One moment he was a limp, dead weight being held up by Bull and the next moment he was springing in the air, all his muscles taut as springs.

Bull whirled in surprise, just in time to meet the full force of Whiskey's kick. Whiskey put everything he had into the blow; it would have snapped the neck of a normal man.

Once she had the gun out, Rhea turned

and shot the policeman standing next to her. The look on his face was one of hurt surprise as he grasped at the hole that went clear through his chest. Then his eyes rolled up and he tumbled to the earth like a felled elephant.

Rhea had never killed a man before and the sight of it nearly made her gag. She turned around in time to witness Whiskey's kick to Bull's head.

The ugly agent managed to partially fend off the blow, but it had still come as such a surprise that he was knocked off his feet and almost into unconsciousness. Whiskey tumbled to the ground nearby.

Despite the fact that his head had just about been knocked off, the agent's training was so ingrained that he managed to draw his own gun before Rhea's shot hit him in the back of the skull, carving off a large slice.

Whiskey rolled to his feet as Rhea hurried over to help him.

"Cut my hands free," he said hurriedly.

"How? With what?" Rhea felt a slight rush of panic.

"Turn the gun on its lowest power and be careful," Whiskey instructed.

While Rhea followed his instructions, Whiskey looked around, wondering where Deadalus was hiding and why he hadn't come to help them.

Rhea finished cutting his hands free and Whiskey picked up the policeman's and Bull's guns, then turned to follow Rhea, who was already running back toward the fence.

When she got out of the main floodlit area, Rhea paused and waited for Whiskey to catch up. Despite his accrobatic kick, she had noticed that he didn't seem to have all that much energy and his eyes looked sort of blurred, as if he was on some kind of drugs. She pondered for a moment whether or not she shouldn't just leave him to his own devices, but decided against it.

When Whiskey had caught up with her, she started off again. She led the way over to the fence and then down along it until they came to the section that she had broken in order to come in. Rhea leaped through and, after a slight hesitation, Whiskey followed suit.

Rhea ran down the embankment and stopped behind some bushes above where the flatboat was beached. The young man joined her, looking around as if expecting someone else.

"Where's Deadalus?" he asked.

Rhea looked at him in shock and surprise.

"You are Rhea, aren't you?" he asked. "Didn't Deadalus come and get you?"

"Are you Whiskey?" she asked, unable to keep the dismay out of her voice.

He nodded, perplexed.

"Isn't Deadalus with you?" he asked.

"No. I mean, he was. Isn't my father with you?" she asked in turn.

"They've got him," he nodded back toward the spaceport.

"Who's they? The Secret Police?"

He grimly nodded again, not looking at her.

"Is that who that man with you was? The ugly one?"

"Yes. We had gotten caught as soon as we left your father's apartment. They had been questioning me," here he perceptibly shuddered, "and were taking me over to the landing craft when you came up."

"So where's my father now?" she turned, looking back at the spaceport as if considering going back after him.

Whiskey quickly put a hand on her shoulder.

"You won't be able to get him. Don't even think about it. You were, we were lucky to get away like we did. They've got him in their ship. We'd never be able to get him."

Rhea looked at him in surprise. She had not intended going back after him but she found Whiskey's pleading attempt to forestall her rather pitiful. It was a bit hard to believe that this scared and helpless-looking young man was the person Deadalus would choose as second in command.

"I wasn't planning on trying to rescue him," she replied. "We can worry about that later. First we've got to go and help Deadalus."

"Help Deadalus? Why? Where is he?"

"He's stuck back in a tunnel," she quickly explained. "We were being chased and he went back with some explosives. The roof partially caved in and his leg got trapped under some rubble. I couldn't move it and he was worried about you blasting off before we could get here. So he insisted that I come and get you."

Whiskey sat down heavily and put his head in his hands. "It's no good," he muttered.

"What? What are you talking about?"

"It's no use even trying. They're too much for us."

"They? Who? What's the matter with you anyway." Rhea stared at the man bent over next to her, wondering if perhaps the Secret Police hadn't drugged him or something.

Whiskey glanced up at the angry and perplexed young lady who was standing in front of him. The news of Deadalus had been too much for him. It was only by thinking that Deadalus had come to save him that Whiskey had been generated into action at all. And now that he found that Deadalus too was caught and in trouble, his heart felt like lead and he again just wanted to lie down and curl up. He had the feeling that if he just lay still and didn't move, nothing bad would happen to him. But if he tried to do something, they would catch him again, and this time they would torture him. The image of the rat gnawing on his hand again filled his mind.

"We can't fight them," he muttered. "We don't have a chance. It will only make it worse."

"Of course we can. Look, you and I just got away, didn't we?"

"But what good did it do? Deadalus is still caught. They still have your father. What good does any of it do?"

Rhea stared at him in disbelief.

"Well if we just sit here crying our hearts out, it won't have done any good, that's for sure!" she snapped harshly.

Whiskey just put his head in his hands and moaned.

Rhea bent over and shook him roughly by the shoulder.

"I need you to help me. You've got to come with me and help me get Deadalus. He needs our help. Can't you understand me? We've got to hurry. We can't just sit around here."

Whiskey shook his head. "You don't understand. They've got these rats. If you try to fight they just stick your hands in its cage. It's not worth it. I told them everything anyway. It's just a stupid game."

Whiskey couldn't control himself and his teeth began chattering with fear. One part of his mind was trying to fight down the emotion, trying to make sense and logic out of his feelings, but the fear was too strong. He couldn't shake the nightmares out of his mind.

Rhea stood up, disgusted.

"You're absolutely worthless," she said bitterly. "How in the world did Deadalus ever get stuck with someone so weak and worthless as you? Why, I myself can do better than you. It's surprising that a man like Deadalus would ever waste his time on you. And now you can't even lift a finger to help him. You're worthless, you really are."

She watched him carefully to see what the effects of her chiding would be. She was hoping that she could goad him into action. But the young man just sat there, mournfully shaking his head.

Rhea sighed with exasperation and looked around. The sky was light now, dawn coloring the horizon. She felt that too much time had been allowed to slip past since she had left Deadalus. She was going to have to get back and help him by herself. This Whiskey character wasn't going to be any help at all. He was evidently scared out of his mind and Rhea didn't have the time or inclination to try and find out what it was that frightened him so. He still had the agent's gun. He'd just have to wait here and lie low until she could get back with Deadalus.

"Alright. You stay here then. I've got to go and get Deadalus."

"Wait!"

Whiskey had jumped to his feet and started after her.

"I don't have any more time. I've got to go back and help Deadalus."

Whiskey grabbed her arm and pulled her around.

"You can't just leave me here!"

Looking in the young man's eyes, Rhea was reminded of a frightened rabbit. Whiskey was evidently terrified at the idea of being left alone.

"I'm going," Rhea replied, shaking loose from his grasp and getting in the boat. "You can stay here by yourself or you can come with me."

She started up the engines.

Whiskey looked wildly about, panicked. He stood there unmoving. Rhea looked at him for a second then started the boat back away from the bank.

At the last second Whiskey leapt into the flatboat.

chapter ten

Deadalus stretched his neck, trying to keep his chin out of the ever-rising water. He had changed his earlier evaluation of his situation. He now believed that this was the very stupidest predicament he had ever been in.

If the piece of the roof that had fallen on his leg had fallen on his head instead, it wouldn't have been nearly so embarrassing. But now he had to sit here, unable to do anything, and wait for this stupid water to drown him. And it wasn't even a decent flood of water. It was just this small trickle that steadily added up. It was just plain silly.

Deadalus had always known that he wasn't going to die of old age. But he had thought that he would go out in some kind of tremendous explosion or fall fighting beneath the overwhelming odds. It was ridiculous that he should end up here being trickled to death.

He thought of Chief Hissler and smiled grimly. At least his uncle would be as disappointed as himself. Maybe even more so. Deadalus laughed at the picture of what the Secret Police chief's face would look like when he got the news that Deadalus drowned all by himself, without any help from Hissler or his ferocious agency.

Deadalus changed the handhold he was using to keep his head above the rising water. He was trying to use just one muscle at a time. In the cold water, he found that his muscles had a tendency to start cramping and, as absurd as he found his predicament, he didn't want to drown before he absolutely had to.

By shifting in his position, he stirred up the water and it splashed up over his mouth. He pulled his head back and away, spitting out the musty taste, and looked for the thousandth time back up the tunnel to the exit.

The spot of sky that shone in was now light blue, indicating that the sun must be up over the horizon. Every once in a while he could hear the sounds of passing boats as the canals came to life with the new day. He briefly considered yelling to try and attract someone's attention. But that would just mean winding up in the hands of the police, or worse. He decided he might as well bear it out where he was and not give his uncle's men the pleasure of torturing him to death.

The water had risen up over his mouth now, and it was all he could do to keep his nose high enough to breathe. There were only a few minutes left.

Deadalus thought he must be going crazy when a minute later he heard someone calling his name. Turning his head, he saw Rhea and Whiskey hurrying down the tunnel toward him.

Rhea helped support his head while Whiskey heaved the rock off his leg, then together they helped him up out of the tunnel. They laid him down inside the boat, which, Deadalus noticed, was a different boat than Rhea had left in.

"You sure cut that one pretty close, guys," he said jokingly. "But I'm glad to see you all the same.

Instead of replying, Whiskey got back out of the boat and started scrounging around the small island for some boards to make a splint with.

Deadalus noticed that there was something strangely wrong with the young man.

"Where'd you get this boat?" he asked Rhea.

"The other was too slow for your friend, so we switched."

While bandaging his leg as best she could, Rhea quickly filled Deadalus in on what had happened since she left, and the circumstances in which she had found Whiskey. She related the incidents as matter-of-factly as she could, letting Deadalus draw his own conclusions as to the cause of his young friend's behavior.

For the moment though, Deadalus was more concerned with the fact that the Secret Police had hold of Rhea's father. That was going to be the biggest problem. Now their task would not be to simply escape, but they were going to have to somehow try and save Pablo. If they couldn't save him, Deadalus thought grimly, they were at least going to have to make sure that he died before the Secret Police could make him talk.

Whiskey came back with two pieces of wood and used them to splint Deadalus's mangled leg.

"So how'd they get you?" Deadalus asked lightly, trying to get the young man to talk while he worked.

"They jumped us the second we stepped out of the doctor's apartment," he replied in a low, peculiar voice.

"Is the doctor still alive?"

"Was the last I saw of him."

"Are they holding him in their ship?"

"As far as I know."

Whiskey's taciturn, almost sullen replies were disquieting. He sounded like a man fated to die. Deadalus didn't like the sound. Something was definitely wrong.

He didn't have time to question the young man though, for before Whiskey even had time to fully tie the splint they heard the roar of an approaching patrol boat.

Whiskey leaped to the controls of the small, sporty boat as Rhea strapped herself and Deadalus in. She handed him back the gun he had given her and then reached up and took Whiskey's from him as the young man jumped the boat into full throttle and they bounced away down the canal.

Whiskey sped across an intersection, right in front of a speeding police cruiser, which swerved violently to miss them until it realized who they were. The wail of their siren rose up in the morning sky, but Whiskey had already dodged around one corner and then another.

Though still not heavy, there was more traffic on the canals than there had been earlier and Whiskey had to swerve around different boats as he sped along. Another cruiser joined in the chase and though the little boat they were in had good speed, Whiskey was still not able to outrun them. In a few minutes of high-speed swerving and sliding around sharp turns, the front cruiser had closed to within firing range.

So that was just what Deadalus did.

He caught the first cruiser by surprise. And though he was fairly certain that his shots hadn't hit anything vital, the boat swerved out of control and plowed into a row of docked boats, flipped over in the air, and blew up when it hit the water.

The next cruiser in line closed in. And they were prepared. This time the police started firing first. Deadalus and Rhea ducked as low as possible, but if any of the policemen's shots came close, it was sheer luck. They evidently weren't trained in running gun battles. And Deadalus and Rhea also had the advantage of being able to see where the police boat was going to go and so could lead their shots. Nonetheless, Deadalus didn't expect either side to do too much damage to each other. He was just trying to give the other pilot something more to think about.

This worked and, when Whiskey turned suddenly down a small canal, the police pilot failed to adjust fast enough and the cruiser passed right by before it could stop. While the big boat was trying to turn around, Whiskey had already taken three or four more turns and had lost them completely.

Whiskey slowed down when he was sure that they weren't being chased. He didn't want to attract any more attention than he had to.

They started down the canal that led to the spaceport and Whiskey saw that it was blocked by three police cruisers. He immediately turned down another canal, but one of the cruisers had spotted them. Its siren went on and they gave chase.

Whiskey once again pushed the boat to full throttle. He made one quick turn and then another, and they suddenly found themselves in the canal next to the spaceport, heading headlong into a police cruiser which was speeding right down on top of them.

Deadalus instantly saw the only way out of their dire situation, and with cool authority, he gave the necessary command.

"Jump, goddamnit, jump!"

chapter eleven

It was more of a tumble than a jump that got Deadalus out of the boat and into the water. As he hadn't even dried off yet, the coldness didn't surprise him. He dove down and was still under water when he felt the two boats collide.

When he came back up to the surface, there was debris everywhere and the police boat was ablaze, sending out thick, pungent billows of black smoke.

The canal was narrow and so, despite his one useless leg, Deadalus made it easily over to the spaceport island and pulled himself ashore. He crawled quickly over to some nearby cement steps, then stopped and looked around.

The smoke from the fire was so thick that he couldn't see very far in any direction. Most likely, even if someone had seen them leap from the boat, they wouldn't have been able to follow their progress after that.

A little way down the shore, Deadalus saw Rhea pull herself out of the water and he called to her, waving her over. She hurried to where he was.

"Have you seen Whiskey?" she asked, sitting down next to him on the steps which were sheltered from the island by a solid bannister.

"Not yet. He did jump, didn't he?"

"I think so. I don't really know."

They both were silent for a minute, their eyes searching the water for some sign of the young man. Soon they saw his head pop out of the water and Rhea ran down to help him ashore.

Whiskey had evidently not jumped from the boat until the very last moment and was slightly dazed from the explosion. Rhea led him over to where Deadalus was crouched and the young man sat down, shaking his head.

Deadalus was meanwhile checking his leg, trying to get an idea as to the extent of the damage. He took off the splint, which by this time had worked loose, and untied the crude bandages Rhea had put around it.

It had started bleeding again from one section on his thigh, but the rest had coagulated. Tenderly, he pressed his fingers down along his shin bone. About four inches from his knee he could feel a hard, sharp protrusion pressing up against the skin. The bone there was split and had only barely kept from poking through the skin. It would have to be snapped back.

"Here, Whiskey, give me a hand with this, will you? Take hold of my foot there and when I tell you, pull on the heel. OK?"

"What are you doing!" Rhea's eyes were wide.

"I have to snap the bone back down or else I'll be hobbling about, my leg dragging behind me like a dead weight."

Rhea looked slightly sick, then turned away.

Deadalus positioned his hands on the snapped bone.

"Alright, pull."

The snapping sound was audible even from where Rhea was sitting.

Deadalus wiped the sweat from his forehead and tied the two wooden splints back on in such a way as to keep the broken bone from moving out of place.

Whiskey was sitting back on his haunches, staring down at Deadalus's leg, his face displaying a turmoil of emotions. Deadalus looked at him curiously.

"So what story did you give them, anyway?" he asked in a light tone, as if they were sitting safely off in space somewhere having a drink.

Whiskey didn't answer, nor would he meet Deadalus's gaze.

Deadalus suddenly reached up and grabbed the young man's head with one hand, and with the other pulled back his eyelid and looked at the white of his eye. Whiskey jerked his head away, but not before Deadalus had seen that there were distinct, thin blue streaks across the top of Whiskey's eyes.

Whiskey glared at him as if he had been struck.

"Calm down kid. I'm not going to hurt you."

Rhea had turned around to watch the exchange with confusion.

"Why didn't you tell me that they put you under a probe?"

"But they didn't!" Whiskey replied bitterly, looking away.

"The hell they didn't. Don't you even remember it?"

"Oh I can remember it alright. There's no way I'm ever going to be able to forget that." The young man's voice was filled with pain and dread. "They had it all ready, but they never had to use it. I broke down before they could."

"What are you talking about? Don't you even know what the probe does?"

"No! How could I? I tell you, they didn't have to use it! All they did was strap it on and threaten me with it and I told them everything they wanted to know. Me! Brave, strong Whiskey! I thought I could withstand any pain they inflicted. Turns out all they have to do is threaten me and I completely break down."

"Slow down, Whiskey. You don't understand."

"No! You don't understand! You weren't there! I answered every question they asked without any hesitation. They had me so scared I was ready to do anything for them. I was like a little kid, about ready to pee in my pants. Look!"

He held up his hand, which was shaking violently.

"Even just talking about it does that to me."

"Will you shut up a minute and listen to me?" Deadalus tried to break in.

"Why? What name could you call me that I haven't called myself a hundred times over? I'm ruined. I'm no good at all for fighting those guys. They don't even have to torture me. All they have to do is pretend . . ." Whiskey shut his mouth and stared at him belligerently.

"They weren't pretending! They did torture you!"

"No they didn't! Don't you listen? You weren't there anyway, how would you know?"

"Because a probe leaves marks in your eyes, goddamnit, or are you forgetting that I used to work for the Secret Police myself?" Deadalus spoke quickly and angrily, trying to get Whiskey to listen.

"You say you don't know what a probe

does, well, I'll tell you then. A probe attaches
to the nerve centers in your brain which
generate fear. They flood those centers with
electrical stimuli, creating any level of fear
that they wish. The probe creates fear, pure
and simple. There's no physical pain, no jolt-
ing agony. But it can, and usually does, build
up such an amount of fear that you die from
it. You literally die of fright. That's what
the probe was developed for. It's actually a
very poor tool for interrogation. Not only
does it usually kill the person before they
can get very much out of them, but it also
fills the mind up so much that they can only
deal with questions in a very simplistic and
literal manner. But you see, the probe hadn't
been intended for use in interrogation. It
had been built as the ultimate form of torture. It kills the person with sheer terror.
Other forms of torture are very crude in
comparison. Pain, in many people just builds
up defiance. And the other forms of slow
agonies are always dependent on what the
particular person is afraid of. With the probe,
you can never miss. All you're doing is stimulating the fear centers in the brain. The
victim comes up with his own images of terror. The victim actually tortures himself to
death."

Both Whiskey and Rhea were looking at
him wide-eyed as Deadalus vehemently de-
scribed the torture machine of the Secret
Police.

"There're thin blue lines in your eyes,

Whiskey. If you don't believe me, ask Rhea. Those lines are caused by an overdose of adrenalin in your bloodstream. One of the side effects of being subjected to a probe."

Deadalus could see that the young man was finally beginning to realize what had happened to him.

"All that fear that you feel, all that terror, you've got to realize that it's not really you. You've got to fight it. You can overcome it if you just keep remembering that they put it there, they put all that fear in your head. You can overcome it if you try hard enough, because it's not really your fear. It was artificially induced. They did that to you with a machine."

Whiskey's mouth was set with emotion, but this time with an emotion that Deadalus was more accustomed to. The young man was angry and determined and ready to go after the Secret Police with his bare hands. Then he remembered something else.

"But I did answer all their questions."

"That's not surprising. What's surprising is that you're still alive."

"But do you think I compromised everyone on the *Orpheus*? I can't remember exactly what the questions were, all I can remember is trying my best to answer them, to tell them what they wanted to know. Do you think I told them about the doctor's information?"

"It depends on what questions they asked and how they phrased them. A person under a probe won't divulge information in a normal manner. They're more than willing to answer your questions, but they can only think in a literal manner, and so if you don't phrase your questions just right, the answers could be very frustrating. But don't worry about that right now. You've got to concentrate on fighting off the fear and horror they've put in you. You've got to keep telling yourself that they were the ones who did that to you, not you. You'll be alright, but you've got to fight it. It will stay with you forever if you don't."

Whiskey nodded, clearly determined.

Relieved, Deadalus began checking their weapons, looking to see just what they had and to make sure that the water hadn't hurt any of it.

Just then they heard the heavy sound of boots on gravel approaching on the walkway above them. They ducked down behind the steps. Deadalus passed one of the guns silently over to Whiskey and held the other one ready.

The sound of boots stopped for a moment and a gruff voice called out some hurried orders.

"Alright, you four men check down that way. You other three come with me. Remember, they're armed and deadly. Shoot first and ask questions later."

chapter twelve

Deadalus waited until he could hear the one smaller group pass on beyond them down the path, then he moved silently up to the edge of the embankment. He looked out and took note of what was going on.

The two groups of policemen, there were seven in all, were working a wide strip of area between the pathway and the canal. There was about fifty yards between the two groups and they were slowly working their way together.

While the one group was still trooping down to its position along the road and the other group was starting down the embankment, Deadalus motioned for Rhea and Whiskey to follow him, and he ran across the road as quickly as he could. With his leg hobbled the way it was though, he ended up moving very slow and was almost spotted by a member of the nearer group who happened to glance up just as they had made it safely into the shrubbery next to the spaceport fence.

Now all they had to do was somehow get by the fence and they'd be safe for a little while. Deadalus was puzzling over the fence when Rhea spoke up, mentioning that she already knew a way to get through. She demonstrated the simple procedure to Deadalus. It was so simple that he almost laughed.

Once inside, they ran over to some bushes at the edge of the pavement and concealed themselves.

"Now what are we going to do?" Rhea whispered.

"It seems to me that our first priority should be to try and get Pablo. You say they had him in their ship with you, Whiskey?"

The young man nodded with a frown.

"What's wrong?" Deadalus asked.

Whiskey glanced briefly at Rhea and then looked back at Deadalus. "You don't think they used that probe on him too, do you?"

"It's not too likely. He's too old. It would be certain to kill him." Deadalus frowned for a moment, considering. "But you never can tell."

"But if they did," Whiskey persisted, "he would have talked, wouldn't he? He would have told them the information he was trying to hide."

"He would have answered their questions. But what they could get out of him would be dependent on what kind of questions they asked him."

"But they would certainly ask him about the information, wouldn't they?"

"Yes," Deadalus conceded, though he didn't like the results such a situation would entail. "But even if they ask him for the information, they might not have asked him why the information was important. Or even if they did find out its importance, they won't have broadcast the information in any manner. They would capsule it and transport it back to Earth as fast as they could. So whether he's talked or not, the information is still on that Secret Police ship. Either way, it looks like that should be the first place we visit."

Deadalus let Whiskey lead the way and he limped along behind as best he could. They made it all the way to where the different ships were parked before they were spotted.

The spaceport, which had been bustling with confusion the last time they'd been in it, was now apparently deserted. Someone with authority had finally cleared everyone out, policemen as well as civilians. With all the milling people gone, the entire area was easily watched over by a mere handful of men in strategic locations.

Mindful of the fact that the field was most likely being watched over, the three dodged their way among the ships in as covert and unpredictable a manner as they could. Deadalus chose to bring up the rear not merely because his leg hampered his speed. He felt better having the other two in front of him where he would always know where they were. Because there was another aspect to their situation that he had failed to mention to them.

If they were unable to get to the doctor to get him out of the hands of the Secret Police, Deadalus was going to blow up the entire ship with the doctor on it. He knew that the doctor himself would have agreed to such a contingency, but Deadalus wasn't sure that Rhea would.

He had explained that the information was important, but he had not revealed to Rhea the true nature of that information, knowing that such knowledge could only be dangerous. And though she had shown herself to be excellent in following orders, Deadalus was not sure how far that would go when it came to sacrificing her father's life. So if the action proved to be necessary, he himself was going to have to carry it out. That was why he was bringing up the rear with a handful of powerful explosives primed in his pocket.

They were spotted soon after they had entered the rows of parked ships. The resistance wasn't too bad at first. A dozen or so policemen came charging in from the front gate. Evidently more accustomed to controlling by threat rather than by actual function, they showed neither organization, training, nor even common sense. Two-thirds of them were dropped in their tracks by Whiskey and Deadalus's marksmanship and the remainder dove trembling for cover.

For a few minutes after that their progress was unimpeded. They made it all the way to the Secret Police's docking spot before they really ran into trouble. And the real trouble was that the Secret Police's ship wasn't there.

Someone had not brought the policemen under better organization. They were all staying under cover and though their shooting wasn't any more accurate than before, there were so many of them it was getting pretty difficult for Whiskey, Deadalus, and Rhea to move. When Whiskey saw that the Secret Police ship was gone, he stopped and waited for Deadalus and Rhea to catch up.

"Now what, captain?" the young man asked after telling Deadalus the bad news.

Deadalus looked around, not overly happy with their prospects.

"Your landing craft is still here," Rhea said.

"Are you sure?"

"I was on that side when we came in. I noticed that it was still there."

Deadalus thought for a minute, now and then firing at the policemen who were circling around the place where they were crouched.

"Well, Whiskey, what do you think? Have you had enough sight-seeing? Ready to go back to the ship?"

"Sounds good to me, captain."

They returned the policemen's fire for a while until Whiskey thought he saw an opening and leapt up, sprinting for another nearby piece of cover.

There was an enormous roar of shooting from the policemen as soon as Whiskey had broken cover and the pavement around the young man was decimated. By some miracle he made it alive over to the other piece of shelter.

Deadalus felt his stomach sink. They must have an entire army surrounding them! With his stupid leg the way it was he didn't have a chance.

The piece of machinery that Whiskey was trying to shelter behind was getting cremated by the police. The young man hurriedly indicated to Deadalus that he wanted to come back. Deadalus put up a good show while Whiskey dashed back across the small open space that separated them. He crouched down next to Deadalus and Rhea, out of breath but unhurt.

"Change your mind about leaving?" Deadalus asked.

"Yeah, I just remembered something. I never got that brandy you promised me."

"What are we supposed to do now?" Rhea

asked, her voice showing a lack of appreciation for the men's humor.

Deadalus sighed. "Not much. Just sit here and wait for them to realize that they've got us pinned down. Then they'll move in and . . . and that's that," he finished lamely.

chapter thirteen

Deadalus, Whiskey, and Rhea crouched back to back, pinpointing their shots. If anyone was keeping score, they were way ahead. But that wasn't going to change the outcome much.

Every time one of the policemen got brave enough to stick his head out, one of the three would blow it off. Eventually they would figure out that they should all stick their heads out at the same time. But so far they hadn't grasped this idea.

"What's taking them so long?" Rhea muttered. "Why don't they just rush us en masse?"

"They're probably waiting for reinforcements," Whiskey joked.

Deadalus laughed out loud at the idea. There had to be nearly a thousand policemen already in the spaceport. But they did behave exactly as if they were waiting for a few more to show up so that they could rush the three who were pinned down.

"Can't you do anything but tell jokes?" Rhea asked exasperated.

"He can sing pretty good," Deadalus put in. "Why don't you sing Rhea a song, Whiskey?"

Whiskey started humming a little tune, then stopped, coughing.

"Oh, I really couldn't, captain. My voice is just so out of practice. Maybe some other time though."

Rhea grit her teeth. "Deadalus?"

"Hmmm?"

"You know, the next time you have the impulse to save my life—don't bother."

Deadalus's reply was lost in the sudden increase in the barrage which was raining down on them.

"Alright," Deadalus called to the other two. "Here it comes."

Deadalus turned around and stuck his gun in its holster.

"What are you doing?" Rhea queried.

"I'll show you." He took out the handful of explosives which were in his pocket. Whiskey too had stopped firing and turned around.

"This really shouldn't work against these kinds of odds," Deadalus explained to Rhea. "But these guys have been so bad so far, who can tell. We let them close in just as far as we possibly can. We don't shoot or move or anything. When they're just about on top of us, I'll throw out some of these explosives. They aren't very big, but they're more powerful than what we've been using, so a lot of their effect will be surprise. As soon as I throw them, we run in the same direction. With any luck we will break through their line. Then it will be just a matter of outrunning them to the *Ezra*. You got it?"

Rhea nodded.

They crouched together, watching and waiting.

The policemen had suddenly seemed to realize that they could move as a group and they'd suffer much less damage than when they tried to move individually. They were closing in rapidly now. First one side then the other. Deadalus watched them and he knew that this last maneuver of his wasn't going to work. There were just too many policemen, and even as incompetent as they were, there was no way that the three of them were going to break through their massive line. They had to do something though. They couldn't just sit there and wait to be slaughtered. He was glad to see that neither Whiskey nor Rhea mentioned surrendering.

The policemen closed in.

Deadalus held the explosives ready and nodded to Whiskey and Rhea. On the next rush.

The policemen started forward.

Deadalus threw the explosives and leapt from cover, the other two close behind him.

The explosives landed in the midst of the

startled troops with a surprisingly loud roar. Deadalus led the way straight for the center of the holocaust.

When the smoke cleared, there were bodies and pieces of bodies all over the pavement. Firing their guns in every direction, they ran through the small space provided in the ranks of uniformed men. They made it cleanly through the front ranks. But that was all.

Those policemen who had been far enough from the explosion not to be panicked by it closed in around them. Deadalus, trying to run a little faster, put too much pressure on his damaged leg and it gave out under him. Whiskey hurried back and helped him to his feet, but a moment later they both had to dive for cover under the barrage of fire.

Rhea joined them and they returned fire as best they could, but the place they were trying to shelter in was too small and too flimsy. They didn't have a chance.

Just then a shrill wail split the air. The sound rose and fell in the unmistakable warning for an air raid.

Everything seemed to stand perfectly still for a moment, all eyes unbelievingly searching the skies. Then, from out of nowhere, there was the sharp-pitched whistle of diving spaceships, and two small landing craft came hurtling out of the sky down at the spaceport.

Deadalus watched in fascination along with everyone else as the two ships made a perfect maneuver, pulling out of their dive at the very last second. Coming in from opposite sides of the spaceport, the two ships raked their lasers across the lines of police officers and peppered the ground with small explosives.

With the sudden realization that they were being attacked, the policemen ran for any available cover, thrown into complete confusion by the buzzing ships.

Rhea and Whiskey helped Deadalus to his feet and together they ran in the direction of the *Ezra*. Deadalus had recognized the attacking spaceships. They were the *Michelangelo* and the *Plutarch* from the *Orpheus*. If he had any lingering doubts about his crew's ability and willingness to fight, they had just been completely dispelled.

The two craft kept diving heartlessly on the panicked ranks of policemen, giving their three comrades on the ground all the protection they needed. The policemen had no alternative but to remain under cover. Their hand weapons were no good at all against the recklessly diving ships. They wouldn't be able to do anything until they had called in some of their own fighting ships, which would take a while. No one ever believed there was going to be an air raid. There probably hadn't been one since the last great war.

Under the continued protection of the spaceships, Deadalus, Whiskey, and Rhea made it to the *Ezra* without any problem.

They had strapped in, checked the controls, and blasted off before the men on the ground were even certain what was going on.

In a matter of seconds they were beyond the atmosphere.

"*Ezra* to *Michelangelo*," Deadalus called over the radio. "Is that you, Jay?"

"*Michelangelo* here. Yeah, captain, it's me. How's it going?"

Deadalus smiled at Jay's drawled reply.

"We here on the *Ezra* would like to extend our appreciation for your timely intervention. How the hell did you find us?"

"Just luck, captain. By the way, you've got three ships coming up on you, about five o'clock."

The warning was unnecessary. Deadalus had seen the chase ships the moment they had cleared the horizon. They were small but quick, and they appeared to know what they were doing. Deadalus watched them as they spread, covering the greatest area of intercept while remaining within range of each other.

"Whiskey, what gun are you on?"

"Port side, ready to go, captain."

"I'm on the other," Rhea chimed in. "How do you work this thing?"

"Just point and shoot," Whiskey replied.

"Do I lead them at all?"

Deadalus, letting Whiskey reply, heard the young man pause as he realized that Rhea was serious.

"No, it's a regular laser. But you've got to backfire in accordance with our speed."

"Is that the red number in the corner of the scope?"

"You've got it. Compensate about one-half degree for each thousand kilometers per second of our speed."

Deadalus watched the enemy ships approach, and when he'd decided the best course of action, he called his other two ships.

"*Ezra* to *Michelangelo* and *Plutarch*, going to try a one-forty-H here. Back me up."

The only possible disadvantage the three chase ships had in attacking together was that they could get in each other's way. No matter how well you planned and practiced, when actually in battle it always came down to split-second judgments of what the enemy ship was going to do. Unless the pilots had fought together for a long time, they could be as much hampered as helped by each other.

Deadalus's maneuver was designed to take advantage of this inherent flaw. He dropped down, bringing his ship into line with the lowest chase ship. He gave the enemy ships half a breath to try to readjust and then he put the ship into a roll and then a tight flip. The result was that the lowest ship overran him, the top ship was unable to shoot without risking damage to the other two, and the middle ship was dead center in Deadalus's missile sights.

Deadalus fired both missiles, then rolled to give Whiskey a shot at the lower ship, which was trying to circle back up below them.

Whiskey's shot missed but Deadalus's went true, blowing one of the chase ships into miniscule fragments. As Deadalus spun the ship gracefully away from the dangerous flying pieces, he felt a resurgence of confidence and power. Now that his movement wasn't dependent on his lame leg, he felt like a fish back in water. He spun the ship into a complicated turn almost playfully.

Deadalus noted that the two remaining chase ships had recovered well. He saw them getting into position to pin the *Ezra*. It was the proper maneuver and was almost a certainty to work. Almost.

The mistake that the chase ships made was that by concentrating solely on Deadalus's ship, they'd momentarily neglected the other two ships from the *Orpheus*.

Deadalus drove his ship up as he saw Jay's ship diving down. The chase ship fired and swerved, but it was to no avail. As Deadalus dodged out of the way, Jay's missile caught the enemy ship from behind.

Looking around, Deadalus saw that the last chase ship was being chased back toward Meer by the *Plutarch*.

"Nice shooting, *Michelangelo*. Now how do we get back to the *Orpheus?*"

"I've got you in sight now, captain," a new voice broke in.

"That you, *Orpheus?*"

"Sure is. And we're going to have to hurry. There seems to be an army fleet in the area."

Deadalus checked the communication channels. There were a great number of ships in the vicinity. And they weren't concerned about keeping themselves hidden either. Deadalus had a pretty good idea who the ships were looking for.

"Alright. *Plutarch, Michelangelo,* let's close it up and get out of here."

"This is McNeace on the *Plutarch.* We've got a problem here, captain."

Checking the screen, Deadalus saw that the *Plutarch* had stopped but had not turned around from where it had been tailing the last chase ship.

"What's wrong?"

"The engines on the port side aren't responding. The cabin pressure fell off. We managed to seal it up, but we can't seem to raise the pressure back to optimum."

Deadalus checked the screen. There were still no other ships in sight.

"*Orpheus,* how far away are you?"

"Five minutes. And we've got company."

Deadalus had to decide. If they moved immediately, there might be enough time to evacuate the crippled landing craft. The crew on the *Plutarch* would be sitting ducks if attacked by the enemy ships. But Deadalus didn't want to sacrifice the landing craft unless he absolutely had to.

"What have you got there, *Orpheus*?"

"Looks like one, no, two C-3 class. Empirical army, by the looks of them."

Deadalus considered. Sounded like just transport ships. Slow and heavy, they would present no problem for the *Orpheus*. But they were too big for the landing craft to fight. And if the *Orpheus* had been spotted, it would only be a matter of minutes before the entire area was swarming with enemy ships.

"*Orpheus*, this is the *Ezra*. I want you to pick up the *Plutarch* first thing. It will take a little work because they're unable to maneuver. The *Michelangelo* and I will distract the enemy's ships while you do that."

"Yes sir."

"Jay? Did you follow that?"

"Uh, sure did, captain. How do you propose we distract them?"

"Just harassment. We aren't going to be able to do them any real damage, but if we can get them to concentrate on us, then maybe the *Orpheus* will have enough time to pick up the *Plutarch*. The most important thing is to make sure that you keep moving at top speed. They're slow, but they've a lot more firepower. And make sure not to get too far away from the *Orpheus*. We're likely to have a lot more company in a few minutes."

"*Ezra*, this is the *Plutarch*. Anything we can do?"

"No. Just sit tight."

They didn't have long to wait. The blimp of the *Orpheus* showed up on the edge of the radar screen, followed a moment later by two smaller blimps. Deadalus took off, the *Michelangelo* close behind him.

At full speed, Deadalus aimed his ship so that it would pass close under the *Orpheus* and come up between it and the two enemy ships. As he closed in, he was able to locate the other ships on the visual. They were just what he had expected, slow, heavily armored army transport ships.

He came up merely yards in front of their noses, firing both rockets simultaneously, aiming for the exposed electronic equipment, the only really vulnerable spots on the heavy ships.

The enemy ships slowed nearly to a halt, more startled than hurt. Deadalus rolled up and away from their return fire. He caught a glimpse of the *Michelangelo* raking its laser across the underside of one of the big ships and then he lost sight of it as he had to dive and twist out of the way of the large missiles fired by one of the army ships.

Deadalus circled around and dove back down on the ship from behind. The other enemy ship had veered off, chasing the *Michelangelo*. Both Rhea and Whiskey were firing their lasers now, but if they did any damage it would only be by accident.

The army ship started up again in the direction of the *Orpheus*, which had come to a stop next to the disabled *Plutarch*. Deadalus dove again right in front of the ship, firing at anything that looked the least bit susceptible.

He must have hit a soft spot. Suddenly the enemy ship came alive, firing rockets and lasers and turning to chase after Deadalus. Deadalus swerved and dodged, leading the army ship farther away from the *Orpheus*.

Checking the screen, Deadalus saw that Jay was flying in erratic circles, the other enemy ship vainly trying to keep up. Deadalus had an idea and sped off in Jay's direction.

The weapons on the small landing craft weren't big enough to really hurt the heavy army transport ships. The enemy ships, on the other hand, were firing powerful long-range missiles. Deadalus straightened the *Ezra* out on a course which would intercept the ship that was chasing the *Michelangelo*. He then slowed up enough to let the army ship get in line directly behind him.

His hands tensely on the controls, he watched the rear viewing screen and waited. The army ship had a straight shot at him and when they didn't immediately fire, Deadalus thought that they must have seen his trick. But then he saw the bright flash that indicated a missile shot.

Deadalus dove and then veered hard to the right. The missiles just barely missed him. Deadalus grinned as he watched the missiles go straight at the enemy ship chasing Jay.

The explosion was not as big as Deadalus had hoped, but it was enough to stop the other ship dead in its tracks. Deadalus watched the ship which had been chasing him hesitate for a moment and then speed off to help its friend.

"*Michelangelo* to *Ezra*. That was pretty good, captain. Now what?"

"I think they're going to be occupied for a while. Let's get out of here."

Deadalus led the way back in the direction of the *Orpheus*. They had gone farther then he had thought, but when they got back, the *Orpheus* still hadn't managed to load the crippled *Plutarch* aboard.

"*Ezra* to *Orpheus*, what's the problem?"

"She keeps getting stuck on the side of the dock, captain. I'm afraid I don't have good enough control up here to move down around her, and McNeace has been trying to work it in but it's not going too well."

"Alright. Let me fly by and take a closer look. *Michelangelo*, you can go ahead and dock."

As Jay maneuvered the other landing craft into docking position on the *Orpheus*, Deadalus drifted down to see what was hanging up the *Plutarch*. He gently circled the other landing craft until he could see what the problem was.

"*Plutarch*, you've got a loose cable. It keeps getting hung up. We're probably going to have to suit someone up and send him out there to guide it over for you."

"We've got half a dozen ships on the screen, sir," came a voice from the *Orpheus*. "Converging rapidly."

There wasn't going to be any time to send someone out to help with the cable. They had to leave immediately.

"OK. McNeace, I'm going to try to push the cable out of the way with the nose of my ship. You hold it steady until I give you the word."

Slowly, Deadalus eased his ship in until the hulls of the two landing craft were almost touching. Then, very carefully, he inched the nose of the ship up. Glancing in his radar screen, he saw two of the enemy ships approaching at full speed. He inched the ship up farther. He couldn't see the cable now, he had to just go by instinct. He eased the ship up another foot.

"Alright, McNeace. Try it now, but take it easy."

There was a thump and the sound of grinding metal as the two hulls scraped together and then the *Plutarch* popped loose and into the hanger.

There was a sigh of relief over the radio. Then a voice called out, slightly hurried.

"Three ships closing fast, captain."

"I see them. Prepare to take off as soon as I get docked."

Deadalus scooted the *Ezra* over to the third docking area, hearing the sounds of the *Orpheus*'s lasers fire as he did. He had barely gotten the craft docked and secured when there was a terrific jolt as the *Orpheus* took off at full throttle.

Before the slow army ships could even turn, the *Orpheus* was gone. A few moments later they were even out of radar range.

chapter fourteen

Deadalus propped his leg up on the side of the console and took a long sip of his drink. It was artificial powdered beer, but it tasted very good nonetheless.

"I propose a toast to Jay, and all the crew of the *Orpheus*," Whiskey said loudly, raising his own cup.

Deadalus grinned across the table at Jay. Jay was tall and lanky, with a long nose that gave a nasal twang to his voice. He was very slow and calm and was not in the least flustered by Whiskey's toast.

"Weren't nothing," the thin man drawled. "I just wish we had some way to keep in contact with you guys when you're earthside."

Deadalus made a mental note of the suggestion. He'd have to do something about that in the future. As it was, the only way that Jay had found them, or even thought to look, was by intercepting messages that were being sent by the locals and the Secret Police ships. The chief's general alert had tipped him off. After having gotten the *Orpheus* out of harm's way, he had come down in the other two landing craft to see if he could help out. It turned out he could.

"We've still got some business to attend to," Deadalus said, interrupting Whiskey, who was telling anyone within earshot exactly what had happened.

Everyone was immediately attentive.

"First, we've got to locate the Secret Police ship. Second, we've got to find out about Doctor Pablo. Third, we have to come up with some plan to stop that information from being taken back to the labs on Earth. If we can't do that, we may as well have just given up yesterday."

The faces around the table lost a little of their good cheer as they once again faced the gravity of the situation.

"About that ship, sir," Jay said. "There was one ship that took off from Meer a little while before we came down. There hadn't been any other air travel all morning, so we were curious about it."

"And?" Deadalus asked impatiently when the other had stopped talking.

"Well, so we kept track of it, is all."

"You tracked it?"

"Uh, yes sir. Still are, as far as I know."

Jay leaned over to the intercom and called down to navigation. In a moment the console screen showed the graph of a ship's progress out from Meer. A short distance from the planet it docked in a mother ship. And then the starship started off. The times and coordinates were all shown.

"That must be her," Whiskey said. "No other ship took off."

"Alright. That solves that problem. Thanks again, Jay." Deadalus found himself being more and more impressed with the abilities of his crew. "Now for our plans. First we've got to get aboard the enemy starship. Then we must find out if Pablo is still alive or not. If he is, we take him and any information they've gotten from him. If not, we must find out what information they've gotten. I'm fairly certain that they wouldn't have beamed the information back to Earth. If they know how important it is, they wouldn't have risked it. If they don't know its importance, they wouldn't have bothered. They've most likely stored it in a safe-capsule for hand delivery."

"Why don't we just blow the starship up?" someone suggested.

Deadalus glanced at Rhea, who was keeping her face completely blank, steadfastly refusing to give in to her emotions.

"That will always be an option, of course," Deadalus replied. "But the very last option. Whiskey, did you happen to see who the captain of the Secret Police ship was?"

"They called him Webern."

"Captain Webern? How nice. He's an old friend from my training days."

"Great," Whiskey said cynically. "Think maybe he'll ask you over for a drink to talk about old times?"

"Not exactly. But the benefit of fighting against old friends is that you know all their weaknesses. I think that's going to come in handy. Now, about that information. If I remember right, Pablo told me that the information could be rediscovered even without his help, because they knew in what general direction he was working."

"But I thought he said there's not much chance that they'd be able to repeat it," Whiskey said.

"He did, but I think he underestimates the resources of the Empirical Secret Police. Either way though, I'd like to decrease the chance of rediscovery."

"But how can you do that?" Rhea asked. "If they already know in what direction he was working? And they would also know what things he had on hand, since it was their lab he was working in. How could you keep them from experimenting and trying to duplicate the process?"

"What I have in mind is this. They're only going to go to all that trouble if they think the outcome is worth it. I'm sure that they're going to be curious about the information at this stage. Even if they didn't manage to get its importance from Pablo, our involvement in the affair will unfortunately spark the chief's interest. If we go in and steal back the information, or even if we just blow up the starship, their interest will be heightened to such a degree that they would for certain make attempts at duplicating the doctor's experiments. But what if they get the information, undamaged and without any problem? What if they follow the doctor's instructions, thinking that they are going to have what the old man keeps calling the most devastating weapon ever created, what if they excitedly do all this and the experiment completely fails? What would they think then?"

"They'd think the old man was off his rocker," Whiskey mused, following Deadalus's reasoning.

"Exactly. If they carefully follow Pablo's instructions and come up with nothing, they'll think that the good doctor must have just been having an old man's fantasies of Armageddon. They'd shelve the whole thing and never think of trying to re-create the experiments from scratch."

"What you're saying is that we should somehow replace the doctor's information with fabricated figures?" Jay asked slowly.

"Right. Or, if possible, just alter some of the key figures so that everything still looks the same but that the results flop."

"Wonderful idea, captain, only it seems nigh impossible."

"Of course," Deadalus grinned at Whiskey's

skepticism. "Everything we've done so far has been."

"Point by point, Deadalus," Rhea broke in. "What if my father is still alive?"

"If he's still alive, they'll no doubt have questioned him anyway. They'll have both him and the information. We grab him and leave them altered info. If your father is dead, then we just alter the information."

"But you said they'd have the information in a safe-capsule. I thought those things were impregnable," Whiskey queried.

"I can get one open. But what we've got to do is come up with some way in which we can read and record on the tape."

"What kind of tape is it?" Rhea asked.

"It's one of those chemical films that you have to process before you can read it. But we can't process it if we want it to look untampered with."

"Could we make a substitute tape and just switch them?" Jay asked.

"That would be asking quite a bit. I don't really think we could get away with that."

"But if it's a chromium film, the development just enhances it really, it doesn't change the actual configuration," Rhea said thoughtfully.

"What are you thinking?" Deadalus queried.

"Well, I was just thinking that you could probably get a computer to reconstruct the information without processing the film."

"But how would the computer read the film in the first place?" Whiskey asked.

"If we sent an alternating current through the tape, the deposits should build up a charge. Then if we develop a magnetic field—here, let me show you." Rhea got up excitedly and went over to the large computer screen and drew up what she had in mind.

Whiskey went over and watched from behind her shoulder.

Deadalus remained seated, sipping at his beer. The technical discussion had quickly gotten above his head. He was just going to have to rely on their expertise to tell him whether or not it could be done.

Rhea was talking quickly, explaining her idea to Whiskey, who watched skeptically.

"The only problem would be the circuitry. It would have to be pretty complex, and I really wouldn't know how to develop it. Do you have anyone who knows something about circuitry?" she asked, turning back to Deadalus.

"You're standing next to the best circuit jury-rigger this side of the Crab nebula," Deadalus grinned.

Rhea looked at Whiskey, somewhat surprised.

"Do you think you could put together the proper wiring?"

"I can build anything you can design," the young man replied somewhat boastfully. "But it's not going to work."

"Why not?"

"Because, for one, this pickup here will

167

magnetize the tape and ruin your whole effort." He pointed to something on the screen.

Rhea looked at it a minute thoughtfully.

"How about if we did this?" She drew something different.

"That would work," Whiskey conceded. "But it calls for a supressor, and we'd have to go halfway across the galaxy to get one."

"I thought you said you could build anything I could design," Rhea challenged.

Whiskey didn't reply, but his jaw got tight as he looked over the rough design.

"Look, I could rig up something like this that would probably take care of that problem." His voice started sounding interested.

They conferred over the diagram on the screen, which was rapidly growing more and more complex as they added circuitry.

When they had discussed and argued over it for fifteen minutes, Deadalus broke in.

"So, what's the conclusion?"

"I think we can do it," Rhea said quickly.

"It won't work," Whiskey said, almost as fast.

"Why not?" Deadalus asked, forestalling Rhea's adamant protest.

"Because even if we do get this crazy gizmo to function, it'll probably melt the tape."

"We don't have to keep it running though," Rhea said, defending her design.

"All I want to know," Deadalus interrupted, "is if it can do what we want."

"If it works," Whiskey replied.

"If it can be built," Rhea shot back.

"Do you think you can put it together?"

Whiskey shrugged. "I guess so."

"And do you think you'll be able to read the tape and make the necessary changes?" he asked Rhea.

"Well, I probably won't be able to read the whole tape or, as Whiskey pointed out, we'd run the risk of melting it. But I think I should be able to read enough of it to do what we want."

"There's a million things that could go wrong with it," Whiskey put in.

"I can't guarantee it, of course," she conceded. "But the idea seems right. We should be able to work it out."

Whiskey started to protest, but Deadalus cut him off.

"If it doesn't work, it doesn't. But we won't know until we try, Whiskey. If we end up just destroying the tape, then that will just have to be the best we can do. I think it's worth the try though. How soon do you think you can have it put together?"

Whiskey shrugged sullenly. "A week. Ten days maybe."

"Fine. Except we'll need it in about two days if everything works out alright."

"Two days! There's no way I . . ."

"Just let me know if there's anything you need," Deadalus smiled as he stood to leave.

"One question, captain," Jay said as Deadalus started out of the cabin. "Just how the hell do you plan on getting onto the SP ship anyway?"

"Through the bedroom window, of course," he replied, smiling at their bemused stares. "But I'll tell you about it later. Right now I've got to pay a call on an old lady friend."

They all exchanged looks of puzzlement as the captain left the cabin.

chapter fifteen

"Hello, captain. Welcome aboard the *Basin-street*." The young lady's smile was distractingly bright.

Deadalus took note of the rest of the lady's distracting details. This was a chore which taxed neither Deadalus's trained powers of observation nor his patience.

The tall young lady who greeted him as he came into the reception room wore a skin-tight outfit of synthetic, silvery gauze. The tight material was completely transparent, serving only to add sparkling highlights to the considerable charms of her large breasts, thin waist, and wide hips. Her breasts, the large nipples pressed flat by the tight outfit, seemed to be staring at him. Deadalus returned their gaze unflinchingly.

"Captain? Is there something I can help you with?"

The young lady's melodic voice dragged Deadalus back from his near-hypnotic ponderings.

"Uh, yes. I'd like to see Madame Em, please. My name is Deadalus."

As she walked over to the nearby instrument panel to check with someone on the intercom, Deadalus noticed she wore a large handgun belted around her shapely waist. He knew that the cold, deadly-looking weapon was no mere ornament. If the lady was like the rest of the girls he had met in Em's employment, she was most likely not only an expert marksman but a skilled hand-to-hand fighter as well.

Deadalus found himself ardently examining the view presented to him as she turned her back to talk over the intercom. He shook his head. He was going to have to try and keep his mind on the business at hand.

"If you'll please follow me, Captain Deadalus, I'll take you to Em," the young lady smiled. "But I'm afraid that you'll have to leave your weapons here."

Deadalus unbelted his handgun and handed it to her. She glanced behind her at the instrument panel.

"I'm going to need all your weapons," she said, and Deadalus realized that they must have some sort of screening device on him.

He wondered just how good the device was as he handed over the half a dozen small explosives he was carrying. Evidently satisfied with the weapons which he had handed over, she deposited them in a drawer and turned to lead him back down one of the long ship corridors. The scanner had evidently not picked up the knife he had strapped to his leg. The knife, made from a special blend of glass, was designed for just that purpose. But it was likely that, even if the young lady had known about the knife, she wouldn't have really cared.

Deadalus followed her down the corridors, which he was familiar with from his other visits. The *Basinstreet* was a well known, high-class bordello. Whore ships had become popular during the last great war. They would follow the army around the galaxy from one battleground to the next. Most of the ships had disappeared when the war was over. But there came along another breed of ships such as the *Basinstreet*, which catered to a different class of clientele. It wasn't really a legal business. Most local governments had laws against prostitution. But the *Basinstreet* and the others like her were always careful to conduct business just outside of the local government's jurisdiction. The Empirical government could prosecute them, but as long as the bordellos were paying huge taxes, they were left unmolested.

Madame Em, who ran the *Basinstreet*, was an old friend of Deadalus's. They had met when they were both just starting out in their respective careers. Deadalus was a rookie agent and Em was one of the new young girls.

The young lady left Deadalus at Em's door, which opened automatically for him. In the center of the cabin was an antique overstuffed couch that seemed to have no place in a spaceship. In the center of the couch was Em.

Wearing a long, loose gown made from some sort of animal fur, her long black hair tied up loosely in a bun, her face mature and beautiful, she sat smiling at Deadalus, looking like anything but a madame of a ship full of prostitutes.

The door closed behind Deadalus with a hush.

"I'm glad to see you're still alive," she said, her voice low and happy.

"You know I wouldn't get myself killed before seeing you again." He stood smiling, looking down at her.

She stood up and kissed him gently on the lips.

"Rumor has it that you're an outlaw now, Deadalus."

"Oh? Well, I guess that puts us on the same side then, doesn't it?"

"Don't be rude," she replied, and playfully bit his neck. "Seriously, Deadalus, from what I've heard, I'm surprised that you risked coming here."

"Why? Are you going to turn me in?"

She laughed. "Not until they offer a sizable reward. But we do get a lot of your old co-workers through here."

"I know, Em. That's really why I came to see you. I have a favor to ask of you."

"Don't they all," Em smiled seductively.

"I didn't mean that type of favor."

"I did." She reached up and licked his ear.

"Uh, Em, do you know a man named Webern? Captain Webern?" Deadalus tried to keep the conversation going while she bit his ear.

"Ummm, I suppose," she replied, running her hands down the front of his jump suit.

Deadalus felt his purpose starting to slip from his mind. He fought to remain in control.

"Will you listen to me? I'm trying to talk to you."

"What makes you think I'm going to do you any favors, Captain Deadalus?" she asked, pulling open the pressure tabs that held the front of his uniform closed.

"Hey! Will you let me talk for a minute? You might remember that about a year ago I saved you from a fate worse than death and you swore eternal gratitude. If you're having trouble recalling it, let me refresh your memory. He was about seven feet tall and there was this tattoo on his forehead . . ."

"I remember. Please don't go into details." She opened up the top of his uniform and bit down on his breast.

"Em! I can't talk when you're doing that."

"Then why don't you shut up?" She ran her hands down his strong stomach.

"What are you trying to do anyway?" Deadalus said, trying desperately to keep control of the situation.

Em paused a moment in her biting and looked up at him.

"Mister, if you don't know what I'm doing, you've been out in space too long."

"I don't have very much time, Em."

"Then quit wasting it."

Em was down on her knees in front of him, pulling his jump suit completely open and running her tongue up along his thigh.

Deadalus couldn't think of a single good argument.

He lifted her up to her feet, stepping out of his uniform, and kissed her. She responded wholeheartedly, snaking her tongue into his mouth and pressing her entire body hard up against his.

She rubbed her stomach and hips against him as he ran his hands down the firm lines of her body. The soft prickling of the short fur gown was extremely stimulating as she rubbed against him faster.

He hiked her dress up above her waist and felt the smooth warmth of her skin as his hands explored her well-formed and exciting body.

She then lifted herself up and wrapped her legs around his waist, slowly lowering herself down onto him until she was fully impaled and wriggling like a fish speared through by a long harpoon.

Em was an expert and she brought them

both to a climax almost immediately. Deadalus rested for a moment, catching his breath. Then he laid Em down on the couch and gently took off her clothes. He made love to her again, this time slow and gentle.

Em smiled at him brightly as he lay on the couch next to her.

"Care for a drink or smoke, captain?"

"A drink would be nice," he said, sitting up. "Have you got any real Earth drinks?"

Em got up and walked lightly over to the instrument panel.

"I've got gin and bourbon."

"No Scotch?"

"No one has Scotch, sweetheart."

Deadalus sighed. "Bourbon would be fine."

Em punched out two drinks and carried them back to where Deadalus was sitting.

"What did you do to your leg?" she asked, indicating the bandage he had wrapped around it just above his knee.

"Busted it up some. Hardly notice it now, though. It's marvelous what modern medicine can do." He grinned at her, sharing an old joke.

"So what's this favor?" she asked, sitting down next to him and decorously crossing her legs.

"I need your help to sneak me onto Captain Webern's ship."

"You know I don't get involved in things like that, Deadalus."

"I know, Em. And you know I wouldn't be asking you if it wasn't very important. I promise you no one will ever know your part in it."

"Deadalus, I'm very grateful for all you've done for me, but you should know that I can't . . ."

"Just listen to me for a minute, OK? It's not really as bad as it sounds."

She sipped her drink contemplatively as Deadalus outlined his plan for her.

"What do you think?" he asked anxiously when he'd finished.

She eyed him calculatingly. "And none of my girls are going to get caught in the middle of this?"

"My word of honor."

Em thought for a moment longer. Then she smiled mischievously.

"It's going to cost you."

"Cost me? What?"

Em smiled, finished her drink, then decorously uncrossed her legs.

chapter sixteen

Captain Webern hesitated a moment, then poured himself another drink. He didn't particularly like the taste of the alcohol, nor its effect. He would have preferred some kind of drug, but that would have meant going to the medic. Drinking he could at least do in private.

After feeling so young and certain of himself all his life, Webern now felt old, worn out, and helpless. He was on his way back to Earth on direct orders from Hissler. The chief had left no doubt as to the captain's fate. He was going to be busted all the way down the line. He was going to end up digging trenches on some frozen asteroid out at the other end of space. He was finished. His once promising career washed up.

When Webern had called Hissler back to tell him that Whiskey had somehow escaped, that the information the young man had divulged under the probe was nearly useless, that the doctor had talked under the probe's pressure but had then promptly died from heart failure, and that Deadalus was still somewhere loose on the planet after having killed one of his agents and slipping right through his fingers, the captain had had little doubt as to what the chief's reaction would be.

Hissler, after informing the captain exactly what he thought of him and of what he thought of his mother and his mother's mother as well, told the captain to proceed directly back to Earth with the little information he had garnered from the doctor. The chief already had other forces in the area to locate Deadalus, forces which, the chief was quite happy to inform him, couldn't bungle the job half as well as Webern had, even if they were all horses' asses. The chief was going to use the doctor's death under torture as an excuse to court-martial Webern. Webern knew it, and he knew that there was not one damn thing he could do to change it.

The intercom buzzed from the bridge, startling Webern out of his half-intoxicated thoughts.

"Captain, we've got a distress signal here from a trader ship that identifies itself as *Basinstreet*. Should we answer it?"

Webern was for a moment too surprised to reply. Then a large grin lit his features.

"By all means, by all means. Find out just what sort of problems this, uh, trader is having. In fact, I'll be right up to take it myself."

Webern couldn't stop grinning as he went unsteadily up to the bridge to talk to Madame Em. He was very familiar with the *Basinstreet* and he knew that whatever kind of trouble they were having, he'd be more than happy to stop and fix it.

After all, he was in no rush to get back to Earth.

"Yes, I'd very much like a drink," Captain Webern smiled and sat down on the peculiar overstuffed couch in Em's cabin.

He had only seen Em previously from a distance. He was pleased to see that she lost none of her appeal on close inspection. His eyes followed her admiringly as she went across the cabin to get his drink and bring it back to him.

"So you think it's fixable?" she asked, handing him his drink.

"Oh, definitely. It will take a couple hours, though. I'll be happy to send a couple of my men over to take care of it for you."

"That would be simply wonderful of you," Em smiled and sat down on the couch next to him. "You know, it's so rare to meet anyone out here who's willing to take time out to help a person. I tell you what, why don't you send all your crew over. My girls have been so lonely, stuck out here like this."

"I'm afraid I couldn't do that."

"But you must let me show you my gratitude," Em pouted prettily.

"What I mean," Webern smiled, "is that I couldn't have my crew leave the ship. But I'm sure that we'd be more than happy to have your girls over to our place."

"Splendid." Em stood up happily. "Isn't it nice when two people can prove to be so useful to each other? I'll have my girls get ready and I'll send them right over."

"Oh, but you must come too," Webern said, standing up close to her.

Em looked at him for a moment as if considering.

"If you insist," she replied seductively.

"I do," Webern grinned. "I do."

The small transport craft from the *Basinstreet* docked on the Secret Police starship where the two dozen crew members were anxiously waiting.

The thirty well-dressed beautiful girls disembarked and were quickly escorted off into the bowels of the ship. Madame Em herself left on Captain Webern's arm, back toward his cabin for some informal entertainment.

At first the sound of laughter and excited voices drifted here and there down the corridors. But quickly this faded away. Even the internal sounds of the ship's machinery seemed to stop as the entire crew left their posts in search of a happier pastime.

When all the corridors were silent and empty, a head popped out from the *Basinstreet*'s transport craft and looked cautiously around. Then, grinning at the sheer simplicity of it, Deadalus turned and motioned for Rhea and Whiskey to follow him.

Deadalus checked his watch as the other two joined him in the airlock. They had an hour and forty minutes at the most. Very likely that wasn't going to be enough time for all they had to do.

First, they were going to have to find the whereabouts of Dr. Pablo. Deadalus had a feeling in the pit of his stomach that his old friend was dead. But if that were the case, the first thing they would have to do would be to verify that. Then they had to locate the safe-capsule with the information. If there was a safe-capsule. And then, they would have to open it, decipher it, change it, and put it back exactly as they had found it. That is, if the equipment Whiskey and Rhea had concocted worked. If not, they were going to have to destroy the information and try to hide their traces so that no suspicion would fall on Em and her girls. And if they couldn't do all this in an hour and forty minutes, they were going to have to abort the mission, sneak back the way they'd come, and start all over again. And there didn't look to be a whole lot of other alternatives except a do-or-die direct attack on the starship itself.

And though the crew of the *Orpheus* had shown their skill, Deadalus still didn't cherish the idea of throwing them up against a fully trained crew of Secret Police.

Rhea and Whiskey, each holding a piece of equipment, stood next to Deadalus, waiting for him to lead the way. With gun drawn and turned down to stun, Deadalus started out down the silent corridors.

The best place for them to operate from would be the communications room. It would likely be as deserted as the other parts of the ship, and it provided access to all they would need. The only problem was that the communications room was clear across the ship from where they were.

There were two ways to get from where they were to the communications room and Deadalus started out in the direction which he considered would less likely be in use at the moment. They moved quickly and silently, Deadalus checking around each corner before they hurried on.

Halfway there they hit a snag. Standing in the doorway to one of the engine rooms was a man and girl, drinking and talking to someone in the room. Deadalus watched from around the corner, but it was evident that they weren't going to be moving. Cursing, Deadalus led the other two back the way they came to try the alternate route.

They hurried even faster, trying to make up for the lost time, and Deadalus almost walked in on a couple. He quickly stepped back and peaked around the corner. On the far side of the rec room, one of Em's young ladies was sitting naked on a table. Sitting on a chair in front of her was one of the crew members. The couple were so occupied that Deadalus considered trying to just cross the room anyway. Had he been by himself, he might have tried it. But there was too much on the line to risk it.

"We're going to have to think of some other way of getting to the communications room," he whispered to Rhea and Whiskey, who were standing next to him, waiting.

"The air ducts?" Whiskey suggested.

"I thought of that," Deadalus shook his head. "But it would take us too long.

Deadalus thought. The design of the ship was the same as the *Orpheus*. He could walk through it with his eyes closed.

"There's a catwalk that goes as far as the food-storage area. We'd have to cross through some of the cabin area to get there though. Why don't we try that."

Deadalus was nearly running now as he led the way back through the maze of corridors. His leg was hardly bothering him at all, but he knew that if he pushed it too far, it would just give out on him.

As they slipped silently through the hallway outside of the sleeping quarters, they could hear voices here and there but they didn't run into anybody. They made it to the food-storage area unmolested and from there passed quickly down the loading catwalk to the communications room.

The room was deserted. Deadalus sat down at the main computer terminal as Whiskey and Rhea set up their equipment. He tied into the ship's information storage bank and traced down the ship's log.

He ran the log back to the date when Whiskey and Pablo had been taken prisoner and then started it forward again, checking each entry for the day. As he neared the end of the day's log without coming across any note of Pablo or his death, Deadalus began to feel a flicker of hope. If they had planned to kill the doctor, they certainly would have done so before they left Meer.

But then, at the very end of the day's log, there was a short note attached recording the death of the doctor, claiming that it had happened while the doctor was under their medical care for an unspecified injury.

Deadalus was overcome with a sudden flood of anger at the confirmation of what he'd feared. He slammed his fist against the side of the terminal.

"Damn those bastards!" he exploded, startling Whiskey and Rhea.

Quickly he regained control of himself and checked his watch. Twenty-five minutes gone. He glanced over at Rhea and saw that she knew what he'd just read without his having to tell her. Deadalus quickly looked away from the immense pain he saw in her eyes.

They had gotten the equipment set up and

Whiskey stood over by the door, keeping watch on the corridor outside. Now Deadalus had to track down the safe-capsule.

The ship's storage bank would hand the capsule to him if he asked for it. But he had to first find out how to ask for it. It was filed away under something and he just had to find out where. It was a process that could take nearly forever. Unless his guesses got lucky.

Deadalus started checking all the places he thought most likely. He punched in subjects and categories, calling for a readout. The computer docilely complied, frustratingly listing all the information contained under each subject. On those categories where the entries were listed chronologically, it wasn't so bad. Deadalus could just glance to the end of the list to see if the capsule he was looking for was there. But in those categories which were listed alphabetically or logically, he had to search through the entire list.

Five minutes passed. Sweat started out on Deadalus's face. Another five minutes. The muscles in his neck started to knot from the tension.

He sat back and took a deep breath, forcing himself to pause and think calmly. He realized now that he should have had both Whiskey and Rhea helping him on this. But if he handed the job over to them now, they'd just start by repeating half the categories he'd already looked through. He forced himself to think the thing through from the beginning. He could feel Whiskey getting impatient and Rhea, sitting quietly by the equipment, waiting in sorrow.

He tried to consider it from Webern's standpoint. Where would he file the information, given that he didn't know the importance of the information nor even really what it pertained to.

Suddenly Deadalus had a hunch. It was almost too simplistic, but maybe his problem was that the computer was acting on too much information. If Webern didn't know what Pablo's information dealt with, there really wasn't that many places for him to file it.

Deadalus punched in the name of Dr. Pablo and there it was. The capsule was listed with its code number. Deadalus sighed with relief and punched the code number in. In a few moments the safe-capsule came clattering down the chute next to the computer terminal.

Basically, a safe-capsule was a small thread of film which had been inserted in an egg-shaped container designed to dissolve the film if anyone tampered with it. To open the capsule properly, you needed a special computer which was coded for that particular capsule. There was virtually no other way to open the capsule without causing the film to be destroyed.

Deadalus's trick however didn't involve opening the safe-capsule. Through many hours of tedious practice, he had learned a method of getting the film back out through the small hole it had been inserted in. It was a delicate process and the smallest mistake would lead to the destruction of the film. But with patience and a steady hand, it was possible.

Deadalus carefully looked over the small capsule to make sure that it didn't hold any hidden surprises and, satisfied that it was nothing more than the normal safe-capsule, he proceeded to delicately poke around in it with a hair-thin wire he had brought with him specifically for this purpose. It took about five minutes of intense, concentrated effort, but Deadalus managed to get the film out of the capsule undamaged.

He handed the film to Rhea, who carefully threaded it into the machine that she and Whiskey had rigged up. She had just managed to get it threaded in when Whiskey turned excitedly from the door.

"Someone's coming! Quick!" he hissed.

They all dove for cover—and found that there was precious little to dive for. Whiskey ducked behind a small cabinet, realized that it wouldn't hide him, and ran over to a tall wall closet. Rhea, being smaller, found a safe spot underneath one of the large consoles. Deadalus couldn't see anywhere to hide and so just quickly ducked behind one of the large sections of electronic equipment.

As soon as he did, the door opened and a man and lady came running in, closing the door quickly behind them. Deadalus peeked from between a maze of wires, his gun drawn and ready. The couple was leaning against the door, breathing heavily and trying to stifle their laughter. It was evident that they were playfully hiding from someone, and the bottle that the man was holding seemed to be the reason for their laughter. In a moment Deadalus could hear more footsteps in the hall accompanied by a loud voice swearing and cursing. The couple held their breath as the voice passed by, and then the girl giggled.

Deadalus kept his gun trained on the agent, ready to fire at the slightest indication that the man suspected something. The closet that Whiskey had chosen to hide in was so shallow that the young man couldn't even get the door shut and it was slightly open. Not only that, but Rhea's equipment was still right in the middle of the floor.

But the crew member seemed to have other concerns at the moment. He opened the bottle, took a long swallow, and then handed it to the young lady next to him. As she drank, he ran his hand up her leg under her skirt. Smiling, the girl closed her eyes and leaned back against the door.

Deadalus bit his lip in aggravation. If the amorous couple chose this room to couple in, they'd really be sunk. He watched as the man's hands explored under the lady's dress, finding something there that seemed to delight them both. The man leaned forward and whispered something in her ear. The lady giggled again and, just as quickly as they'd come, they left.

Deadalus waited a full minute before moving out from behind his hiding place. He motioned for Whiskey and Rhea to come on out as well.

"Let's hurry up and get this over with before we have any more company. Whiskey, you give her a hand with it. I'll keep watch."

With Whiskey's help, Rhea managed to accomplish the task in a short time. The equipment that they had rigged up didn't work perfectly and she was unable to read the whole tape. But it worked well enough to get done what was needed.

Deadalus carefully put the doctored film back into the safe-capsule and put the capsule in the return chute. It was whisked back to the storage tank with a sound that sounded to Deadalus like a great sigh of relief.

They picked up their equipment and carefully hurried back down the catwalk the way they'd come. They passed through the food-storage unit and had almost reached the transport ship when Deadalus suddenly stopped.

Whiskey automatically drew his gun at the captain's abrupt movement, but Deadalus just waved it down with a smile.

"You two go on and wait for me in the transport craft," Deadalus said, turning back the way they'd just come.

"Why? Where are you going?" Whiskey asked, obviously puzzled.

Deadalus just waved them on.

"I'm going to get you a surprise," he said, then hurried down the corridor, leaving Whiskey and Rhea to stare in utter confusion.

chapter seventeen

Deadalus poured out an inch of the orange brandy, then passed the bottle over to Jay, who poured himself some and then passed the bottle on to Whiskey.

They had gotten away from Webern's ship without a hitch. As far as Deadalus could see, the Secret Police didn't suspect anything, and never would. He was certain that Captain Webern would never report about Em and her girls coming on board. There was no way for anyone to figure out what had gone on. There was nothing to indicate to them that anything at all had happened.

Except maybe the brandy. Webern would no doubt have to answer for that. And the captain would no doubt blame his crew.

It was for the brandy that Deadalus had

gone back at the last moment. He had seen cases of it as they passed through the food-storage unit on the enemy ship, but it hadn't really sunk in until they had almost left. And it wasn't until they had brought it back and opened it up that they had seen that the bottles were all labeled for the private use of one Chief Hissler.

That just made a sweet drink all the sweeter.

Deadalus had another glass of the ill-gotten brew and listened as Whiskey and the others joked and laughed, in buoyant good spirits brought on by the difficult mission being accomplished and over.

But Deadalus didn't feel that the mission was either accomplished or over.

Even with the brandy, Deadalus couldn't suppress his bitterness over the death of Dr. Pablo. Pablo had been a good man and a close friend. He had deserved a better fate than to be tortured to death. The memory of his friend just added another stone to Deadalus's already heavy hatred for Hissler. And he knew that he would probably never be able to pay the Secret Police chief back properly. But he sure as hell was going to try.

Deadalus finished his drink and then left the others to their merriment. He didn't want his heavy mood to put a damper on their spirits. Besides, there was still the problem of Rhea.

Deadalus hadn't seen the young lady since

they had gotten back to the *Orpheus*. He suspected that she had gone to her cabin to be alone with her sorrow over her father's death. Deadalus didn't really want to disturb her, but he needed to talk to her about what she was going to do. She couldn't go back to Meer, that was certain. But Deadalus had a number of close friends on other planets who he was sure would be more than willing to take her in and help her along. And Deadalus would make sure that she had everything she needed and that she never again came in harm's way. To see her safe and secure was the least he could do for his friend Pablo.

When she opened the door of her cabin to let him in, Deadalus was somewhat surprised. He could see from her eyes that she had been recently crying. But there were no tears now. Instead, her jaw was set with an angry determination.

He looked at her for a moment, suddenly uncertain of what to say.

"I'm sorry about your father, Rhea."

"I know you are. But there was nothing that you could have done. You tried your best. It wasn't anyone's fault, really. Except Hissler's."

Deadalus watched her face as she spoke, her eyes reflecting all the strength that he'd come to know of her in the last few days. He felt a surge of respect for her.

"Listen, Rhea, I wanted to talk to you.

Have you ever heard of the planet, New Sunland?"

Puzzled, Rhea looked at him and shook her head.

"Well it's a large planet kind of on the fringe of the hospitable belt. It's not primitive or anything, but it's far enough away that it doesn't get bothered too much by the Empirical government. I've got a good friend there and I was thinking that you could stay with him and his family until you could get settled down."

She looked at him in utter confusion.

"What are you talking about?"

"Well, you must know that you can't go back to Meer."

"Of course I know that."

"And, well, I was just trying to think of some place safe where you could go. I didn't know if you knew anyone on any other planet . . ." Deadalus stopped at the look of utter disbelief that had come over her features.

"You must be out of your mind! If you think I'm going to let you tuck me away on some safe little planet, you've had too much to drink!"

It was Deadalus's turn to be confused.

"Surely you realize, Rhea, how much danger you're in from the Secret Police? You must see that . . ."

"Danger? Have I shown myself to be someone who would spend her life running from danger?"

"No, of course not. That's not what I meant."

"Then why in the name of the galaxy do you think I'd be content to spend my life hiding?"

"The last thing your father said to me was to take care of you, and that's just what I plan to do. I'm going to make sure that you're safe, somewhere the Secret Police won't be chasing you."

"I can take care of myself, Captain Deadalus, thank you. Or maybe you haven't noticed. Maybe you've forgotten who it was who got Whiskey to get you out when you were stuck in that tunnel?"

"I know you're a quite capable young lady, don't get me wrong. I was just offering to help you."

"Help me! You want to stick me away on some planet, fine help that is!"

"Well, what do you want then?" Deadalus exploded, exasperated.

"I want to stay here on the *Orpheus*."

Deadalus looked at her, astounded.

"Absolutely not."

"Why?"

"Because the *Orpheus* is the most dangerous place in the entire galaxy for you to be, that's why!"

"I don't care! I don't want a safe little hole to crawl into! Sure the *Orpheus* is dangerous, and that's because it's the only place where I can actually do something to get back at Hissler!"

"Rhea, I know you're upset. But you can't just take on the whole Empirical Secret Police just because of this."

"Why not? Isn't that what you're doing? Isn't my pain as much worth fighting for as yours? Do you think you're the only one who wants revenge against Hissler?"

"Of course not. But this is my profession, this is what I've been trained to do."

"I'm as capable as any man in your whole goddamned crew, *captain*. Don't be fooled just because I'm a female. That doesn't make me any more willing to sit back and let them get away with this. Haven't I proven that I'm willing to take all the risks? Haven't I shown that I was capable of anything you asked? I've got just as much right as you or any of the others to fight!"

Rhea stood half a foot away, glaring furiously into Deadalus's eyes. Deadalus stared back at her, momentarily dumbfounded.

Then he grinned and extended his hand.

"My mistake. Welcome to the *Orpheus*, Rhea. I'm proud to have you with us."

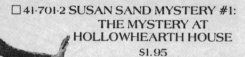